Firebird's Snare

Book 2 of the Pipe Woman's Legacy

Lynne Cantwell

hearth/myth

Table of Contents

How we got here

Don't believe anything my sister tells you.

Well, okay. Maybe that's unfair. Her story of what happened with Veles, the god in charge of the Slavic underworld, is true as far as it goes. She did believe He visited her in her dreams. She did get dragged up to Alaska when her new BFF, Rafe, needed to confront his brother about Veles. Rafe is allied with Raven and his mother is allied with the Tlingit goddess named Bear Mother. All of that is true.

And no doubt about it, Rafe's father was a scumbag and deserved to die. That part, too, went down pretty much as Sage said it did.

But she makes it sound like it was my fault that Hilary's kappa released the water from the catchment basin and caused all the chaos after that. And it wasn't. Enkou was...

What? Oh, sorry. You have no idea what I'm talking about, do you? See, this is the problem with being a sacred clown – you have to do everything backwards. I always launch into stories at the end, assuming everybody knows what I'm talking about, when I'm the only one who knows how things turn out.

That's part of being a sacred clown, too. I have the misfortune of knowing the future – except for the stuff I'm most interested in: the events that directly affect me. When I'm going to be involved, I can see trends, but not specifics. It's like viewing the future through a two-way mirror that's all fogged over. I could tell you whether Sage will indeed save the world in the end, just as our great-grandfather told her she would. I will tell you that Rafe and Hilary – and that annoying kappa of hers – will be involved. But since I'm going to be involved, too, I can't see exactly what we're going to do.

Which is why I have to let Sage tell most of the story.

This is why I make so many jokes. Because otherwise, I'd be pounding holes in all the walls in frustration. Better to laugh than to go around with bruised knuckles all the time, right?

Oh. Sorry. I'm Webb Curtis. Well, actually, Webb is just a nickname – my full name is Andrew Joseph Curtis. I'm named for both my grandpa Drew Sauvage, who's a Lakota Wolf Dreamer – he's going to be involved in saving the world, too, by the way – and my father, Joseph Curtis, who started out being Guardian to Naomi Witherspoon and ended up marrying her. Which was a good thing, as she was already pregnant with Sage. Although I have no doubt that Mom would have been able to manage just fine as a single mom.

On the other hand, we're talking about Sage here, and their relationship has always been kind of rocky. So maybe not.

Anyway, there's a little bit of a question about our origins, Sage's and mine. Legally and biologically, Mom and Dad are undoubtedly our parents. But on a different plane, Sage and I are also the offspring of White Buffalo Calf Pipe Woman, who's a Lakota goddess, and that noted Trickster, Coyote. So nobody in our family seemed surprised when Sage was able to scream up a thunderstorm while she was still in diapers – or when I started knitting spontaneously at the age of three.

Yeah, knitting is my superpower. Big cosmic joke, right?

Anyway, getting back to what I was saying about Enkou: That kappa is a free agent. Not even Hilary can control him. Every time she turns her back on him, he's off creating some mischief, unless she's been able to get him to promise that he will never do it. And he's a master at finding loopholes in the promises she does manage to get him to make.

Which sucks for Hilary, because she's great. She doesn't deserve the complications Enkou causes for her. We talked about it that time when we were waiting by the catchment pond in Nav, the Slavic underworld, while up above us in the real world, Rafe's scumbag father was trying to turn him into a giant talking slug.

"How did you get mixed up with Enkou, anyway?" I asked her.

"You know my parents are Japanese immigrants, right?" she said. I hadn't until that moment, because Sage hadn't bothered to tell me. But it made sense. Hilary Takahashi was tiny, and she had black hair and Asian facial features. Not that I can tell Asians apart, but she definitely looked Asian to me. "Well, Enkou came to America with them. Or he found them after they got here. The story appears to change." She also had a cute Southern accent, which was fun to listen to.

"I know how that works," I said, thinking of my own family. Someday, my mother will write a memoir, and that will become the official story, but I expect she'll sanitize certain things for mass consumption. And knowing Mom, she'll make herself out to be a tiny bit more of a hero than maybe she actually was. That's part of why Mom and Sage are at odds so often – Mom forged the peace in heaven, more or less, but she knows that Sage is destined to save the Earth, and I think it kind of pisses her off.

Anyhow, Hilary went on to explain that she was North Carolina born and bred. She grew up in Durham, where her father did some kind of programming whiz-bang thing for Qualcomm and her mother worked for UNC Health Care. They had a typical suburban house in a typical suburban housing development, complete with one of those water features that acts as a catchment pond to guard against flooding. Enkou took up residence in the pond and got into all sorts of mischief that the neighborhood kids largely took the fall for. But when Hurricane Hubert dealt that glancing blow to the Carolinas in '23, every neighborhood was flooded but theirs.

"As I got older," she said, "he kind of took a shine to me. When I decided to come to CU for college" – she was talking about the University of Colorado at Boulder, which my sister and Rafe also attend – "I could tell he was upset. But I never dreamed he'd follow me here."

"But he did."

"Yeah." She sighed. "And he's been nothing but trouble ever since."

"He's a Trickster," I said. "Trouble is what they do."

"You can say that again." She looked around, and then stood up to scan the area. "Where did he go, anyway? Enkou-san!" she called, and added a few words in Japanese that sounded a whole lot like, *You'd better get back here right now or you're in big trouble!*

I stood up to help her look. I figured he wouldn't be too hard to spot. He might be short, but his appearance is distinctive: he looks like a duck-faced turtle with a bowl of water sunken into the top of his skull.

Anyway, while we were scanning the area for Enkou, we noticed that the water level in the giant reservoir – the one we were supposed to be guarding – was dropping. It didn't take a genius to figure out what was happening. Sure enough, Enkou had taken it upon himself to dive down to the bottom of the tank and pull the plug.

Which was sort of okay. I mean, Sage and Rafe had wanted us to pull the plug. Just not necessarily right that second.

It would have been really good to know that we didn't need to pull the plug at all. The World Tree, whose roots stretched to either horizon far above our heads, had sent down a taproot to the reservoir. If we had just left well enough alone, the taproot would have sucked up all the water and added it back into Earth's atmosphere a little bit at a time. It turns out that regulating Earth's climate is part of the World Tree's job – besides supporting the gods' world above, sheltering the Underworld below, and giving humans a place to live in the middle. But Hilary and I didn't know that. So we kept moving the root as it snaked toward the reservoir.

Maybe that's why Enkou took it upon himself to pull the plug. Maybe he decided we were too ignorant, or too inept, to let Nature take its course, and that an inundation was better than no fresh water at all. Which is about where things stood on Earth, thanks to Rafe's father's henchman channeling all the precipitation and snowmelt in the Northern Hemisphere into the reservoir that the three of us were supposed to be guarding.

Whatever Enkou's reasoning, the end result was that all that water came back at once – as snow. The whole Northern Hemisphere became frozen under ten-foot snowdrifts. That was okay in my parents' neck of the woods – we're used to big snows in

Colorado – but places like Acapulco and Mumbai and the Sahara had no idea what to do with it. The top half of the world chilled dangerously overnight. People died. So did animals. So did crops.

The tropical areas recovered from the cold the fastest. But then all that water had to go somewhere.

To say that Enkou had caused a crisis of worldwide proportions would be an understatement.

I'll let Sage take the story from here. She's the scientist, after all. She's an environmental engineer in training, and a damned fine one, if my sources are correct – and they always are. And she's got a team that understands all that scientific stuff. Rafe's field is environmental studies, and Hilary's a whiz-bang programmer in her own right. The three of them have the chops to solve the problem – no question about that.

But first, they're going to have to run an official gauntlet. And then they get to explain to the New World News Network how they got the Earth into this mess.

Good luck, big sister. You're going to need it.

Chapter 1

When Rafe and I got off the hypersonic plane at Denver International Airport, we thought we were going to go right back to our lives as if nothing had happened.

Boy, were we wrong.

I mean, sure, everything was still covered in snow. And when I say covered, I'm not kidding. You know that old photo that gets posted online every winter where the snow on either side of the road is taller than a tour bus? That's pretty much how everything looked everywhere – in Anchorage when Rafe's mom drove us to the airport from his house, on the tarmac in both Anchorage and Denver, and all the land we could see from the air. Mountains, valleys, towns – everything was buried under a massive blanket of white. It looked really pretty from the air.

Oh, come on. I'm not a total idiot. Alaska does have internet access, and I knew the tropics were having trouble digging out. I also knew people in temperate latitudes around the world were dying from the sudden cold. But it's one thing to see video on the news, and another thing entirely to have a couple of armed soldiers stop you as you step off the jetway. Especially when the whole thing wasn't really your fault.

"Sage Curtis?" one of the soldiers barked as he stepped into our path.

I stopped in surprise, and Rafe bumped into me from behind. Rafe had been doing pretty well at staying upright – especially given that he'd been comatose, with a disgusting iceworm stuck in his head, until just a few days before – but the travel had worn him out, and I was sure he just wanted to go home and go to bed.

"Yes?" I said. Then I stepped aside, realizing we were blocking the jetway exit and holding up the other passengers.

"Raphael Orloff?" the soldier went on, looking at Rafe.

"Present and accounted for," he said, with a sloppy salute.

I threw him a panicked look and turned to the nice man with the gun. "Please excuse him," I said in some haste. "He's had a rough couple of weeks."

Thank goodness the soldier didn't seem put out. All he said was, "Follow me, please," and turned on his heel to head out into the hallway between the gates. Rafe and I shrugged and fell into step behind him. The second soldier fell in behind us.

It was late, so the airport wasn't crowded. But still, our little procession drew some looks. "Um," I said, "we're not under arrest, are we?"

Neither of the soldiers responded.

Rafe looked at me sidelong and said in my head, *They didn't handcuff us.*

True enough, I replied the same way. We had discovered this mind-to-mind communication trick just a few weeks before, while he was teaching me how to fly. And when I say "fly," I mean fly like a bird flies – he's allied with Raven and I'm allied with Thunderbird. It's a long story why I was just learning now, at the ripe old age of nineteen.

So we could probably leave any time we wanted to, he went on.

I glanced back pointedly at the armed soldier behind us. *You want to try it?*

He shot me a mischievous grin. *I bet if we shifted, we could get away before they figured out what to do about it.*

I was just about to reply when the soldier in front of us stopped abruptly before an unmarked door. He knocked twice, opened the door without waiting for a response, and motioned us inside.

As soon as I saw who was waiting for us in the room beyond, I sent to Rafe, *No bet.* Aloud, I said, "Captain Warren? What are you doing here?"

Captain Darrell Warren rose from the folding table he'd been sitting behind and came toward us. "You can call me Darrell. I'm a civilian now." He shook hands with me, his grip firm. "Good to see you, Sage. And this must be Raphael."

"It's Rafe," he said, shaking hands in turn. Darrell slipped him a business card, and I watched Rafe's eyebrows shoot up as he read it.

"Like I said," I told him, with some satisfaction. Then I turned to Darrell. "He tried to bet me that your guys wouldn't be able to catch us if we shifted."

"Ah," Darrell said with a grin. "Nope, sorry. My unit has a fair amount of experience with that sort of thing."

Darrell was a friend of my parents'. I'd met him in Washington, D.C., as my family joined forces with him and some of his friends to defeat Lucifer and keep the Earth humming along the way the gods wanted it. That was before Darrell had formed the quasi-military government agency he had been heading up since then. I didn't know a lot about it, but I knew it had something to do with keeping rogue gods – as well as rogue humans – from disturbing the peace the way Lucifer had. Darrell was perfect for the job. Not only was he a former Navy SEAL – and still built like one, I noted appreciatively – but he was also a Potawatomi Indian shaman who had a bit of shapeshifting ability himself.

Rafe was still looking at Darrell's business card. "What does JAF-H/D stand for?"

"Joint Assault Force Hominid/Deific," said a smug voice behind us. "I thought it up myself."

"Nanabush!" I cried, and crossed the room to give Him a hug. Darrell's god was dressed in buckskin, as usual. His eyes bugged out and His rabbity ears stood straight up in alarm when I put my arms around Him.

"Oh, relax, You old faker," said Darrell fondly. "And You did not think it up. I did."

"Well, I helped," He grumbled. Then His tone brightened. "Hi, Sage. You've grown since the last time I saw you."

"I would hope so," I said. "The last time You saw me, I was, what, twelve?" I turned back to Darrell. "Do Mom and Dad know you're in town?" He and his wife, Tess Showalter, had come out to visit us a handful of times. Usually their friends Robbie and Sue Duckworth came then, too.

"No, and I'm afraid it's going to have to stay that way," Darrell told me. "This is an official visit."

"Clandestine," Nanabush said, hiding most of His face behind His generously fringed sleeve. "Cloak-and-dagger stuff. Need-to-know basis."

Darrell rolled his eyes and continued, "I wanted both of you to know that the government very much appreciates your actions on behalf of the Earth a few weeks back. I know it wasn't easy, and involved a measure of personal sacrifice. Especially for you, Rafe." Darrell laid a hand on Rafe's shoulder. "We'd been watching your father's operation for some time, but we didn't think it had reached a boil-over point. Obviously, we were wrong. I'm sorry."

"It's okay," Rafe said, but his eyes misted over. I glanced away to give him a moment of privacy.

I knew his feelings for his dad were complicated. Ben Orloff had been the one to implant the iceworm in his head. When we cornered him, he gave us a box of syringes loaded with a useless antidote, and then killed himself. Rafe would have been dead if the goddess Brighid hadn't been called in to heal him.

But still, Mr. Orloff had been Rafe's dad. And while he mourned the father he had loved, he also harbored a newfound hatred of the man. We'd talked about it in Anchorage, while Rafe was recovering from his brush with death. "I don't know, Sage," he had said. "I knew Dad was preoccupied with his job. He was one of those guys who only paid attention for a moment, you know? You'd ask him a question and his response would trail off partway through, and you just knew he had stopped thinking about what you'd asked him because he'd gone off on some unrelated tangent in his head."

I knew of at least one Environmental Engineering professor who had the same inability to have a conversation outside of his own head. Everybody avoided taking his classes. The material was notoriously difficult, and unless you got a decent teaching assistant for your section, you were pretty much going to be toast.

"But I always knew he loved me," Rafe said. Then he huffed a rueful laugh. "Or I thought I knew he did. Maybe I was wrong, all those years. Maybe he never loved me at all." He lay quietly for a moment. "I wonder whether he ever loved Paul."

"I'm sure he loved both of you," I said, although privately, I wondered. Paul and Rafe were born twenty years apart and had different mothers. Paul seemed to hate Rafe, and Rafe thought it was because his mother was Tlingit. But that was just conjecture on Rafe's part. If his mother knew the real reason, she wasn't telling.

I turned back to Darrell after a moment and said, "So you pulled us in here just to apologize? You didn't have to bring in an armed guard for that, you know. You could have just sent us an email or something."

Nanabush snickered, but Darrell barely cracked a smile. "Of course not. There's more." He moved back to the folding table. "Have a seat."

I slipped my fingers into Rafe's hand and squeezed. He blinked to clear his gaze and squeezed back. Then we sat down opposite Darrell.

He had put his hands flat on the table and was staring at them as if he didn't quite know how to begin. Then, abruptly, he cleared his throat and looked straight at us. "While the Earth is grateful to you both, your actions have created a problem."

I felt my face get hot. "The snow."

"The snow," he confirmed. "Already, we're starting to see the effects of this massive world-wide weather event."

"I know people are dying," I began.

"Not just people, Sage. Livestock, too. And crops. The world's food supply is in jeopardy."

Nanabush popped in, perching on the edge of the table next to me. "You might say humanity will soon be in a world of hurt," He said with a wink.

"We're really sorry it happened," Rafe said. "But it's not our fault."

"It's Webb's," I said darkly, voicing the accusation that had been simmering in my head throughout Rafe's convalescence. "He and Hilary were supposed to keep an eye on Enkou, and they didn't."

"I'm not here to assign blame, Sage," said Darrell. "What's done is done. I'm not going to hold anybody responsible for the kappa's actions. He's a Trickster, and I know from first-hand experience that Tricksters do whatever They want." He threw the god a disgusted look, and Nanabush threw back His head and laughed in delight.

"So then what's this all about?" Rafe asked as Nanabush trailed off in giggles.

"We need to work toward mitigating the damage," Darrell said. "Near the equator, the world is already starting to warm up again. The snow will melt relatively quickly, and the total impact on life there should be minimal. But the runoff…"

"Is going to raise the sea level," Rafe said, sitting back in sudden understanding. "At least in the short term. It'll cause massive flooding all over the world."

"But in arid climates, won't the snow mostly evaporate?" I asked, thinking furiously. "Wait. That will overload the atmosphere with water vapor. It will make climate change way worse. Oh, my gods." I turned to Rafe. "We've got to *do* something. And we haven't got much time."

"There might be a way," Darrell said, and we turned to him as one. "While you were recovering, Rafe, Dr. Raymond from CU contacted me. It was actually his idea to bring you two on board."

"Why us?" I said. "It's not like we covered ourselves in glory the last time."

"I believe he said you know the players."

Rafe and I traded a look of dismay. "Oh, no," I said. "I am *not* going back down to Nav."

"Even to save the Earth?" Nanabush asked.

I gave Him a hard look. "That's not fair."

He shrugged. "Nobody ever said life was fair. Not even the gods."

I closed my eyes and sighed. Then I looked at Rafe, who was leaning on the table with his head down and his shoulders slumped. "Look," I said to Darrell, "it's late. I'm really tired from the trip, and he's" – I hooked a thumb at Rafe – "just about to fall over. Can we sleep on it?"

Darrell sat back. "Of course. But don't take too long to decide. You said it yourself – we don't have much time." He stood, and Nanabush shot off the table and stood at attention next to him. Then He winked at me, which made me smile.

"When do you graduate?" Darrell asked me as Rafe and I got to our feet.

The question caught me off-guard. "Not for another two-and-a-half years. But then I'll have a master's. Why?"

He ignored my question. "Rafe, how about you?"

He nodded tiredly. "Same-same."

"Well. If you two can pull this off, I can guarantee you both a job with my agency after graduation." Before I could respond, he handed me one of his cards. "This number is a secure line. I always answer it. If you have any questions, don't hesitate to give me a call."

"All right," I said.

"Oh," Darrell said, fishing in his pocket. "There was one other thing I was supposed to tell you." He extracted from his wallet a different business card – this one prominently featuring the NWNN logo – and handed it to me. "Tess wants to talk to you."

I looked up at him in surprise. "Why?"

"She wants to interview you, of course," Nanabush said brightly. "You two are international heroes!"

Chapter 2

I lost Tess's business card somewhere between baggage claim and catching the train to Boulder. I swear I didn't mean to do it, but I was juggling a lot of stuff — a backpack, a suitcase, Rafe's suitcase, Rafe — and it must have just slipped out of my hand somewhere along the way.

Darrell's card, however, I stowed securely. He had promised us a guaranteed job after we graduated. I wasn't about to throw that opportunity away.

Of course, we had to jump through a few hoops before we could collect on those guaranteed jobs. And the very first hoop was waiting on my phone after we got on the train. It was an email from Dr. Raymond: *Crisis mode. Please reply as soon as you are back in town.*

Rafe was looking blearily at the same message on his phone. Then he sighed and stuffed the phone back into his jeans pocket. "You're not going to reply?" I asked.

He wrapped one arm around me and dropped his head to my shoulder. "We're not back in town yet."

"Good point." I leaned my cheek against the top of his head and tried not to doze off myself. One of us had to stay awake, or we'd miss our stop and end up halfway to Eldora.

The next morning, I sat at the dinette, shoving cereal into my mouth while studiously ignoring the *you have mail* chirps from my phone. Kerry stumbled into the kitchen and got herself some coffee. "Hey, you," she said. "How was Alaska?" She had already been in bed when I'd come in the night before.

"Pretty freaking crazy," I said between bites. "How's Stoner Boy?"

She paused in the act of pouring her coffee. "That's unfair."

"Sorry," I said, although I wasn't really. Stoner Boy, a.k.a. Jeff, was the guy who had led campus police to Enkou by taking an unauthorized photo of him – in my bedroom.

"You know I stopped seeing him," she said.

I put down my spoon. "Actually, I didn't know. But I'm glad to hear it."

"Of course you are," she said bitterly. "Because you know everything."

I blinked. "Where did *that* come from? Look, Kerry, I'm sorry we haven't had much time to hang out this semester, but –"

"Oh, we've had plenty of time," she said with a harsh laugh. "Or at least, *you've* had enough time to breeze in and pronounce judgment on the way I live my life, and then run off again to be a hero." She flung up a hand and glared at me.

I stared at her. "I don't..."

"Oh, yes, you do," she said. "You always do. I quit seeing Jeff because he was a loser, just like you said. And I should have talked to Webb much sooner. I'm sorry I've fucked up your life. All right?"

I didn't know what to say.

My phone chirped yet again. "Someone must be desperate to talk to you," she said, almost sneering. "Don't you think you should answer them?"

I was still too surprised to react. But when it chirped once more, she pursed her lips and shook her forefinger at it. Slowly, I picked up the offending device and looked over the last five or ten messages. "Shit," I muttered. "I'm late for a meeting."

"Of course you are," she said, and stalked down the hall with her coffee. Her bedroom door slammed shut a moment later.

I knew I should go after her and find out what she was so upset about, but I didn't have time. Instead, I dumped the rest of my cereal in the sink and went to throw on some clothes.

Twenty minutes later, I arrived at Dr. Raymond's office in the Cristol Chemistry Building, out of breath. "Sorry I'm late," I panted as I flopped into a chair. "I would have been here sooner…but I had to stick to the sidewalks…because of the snow."

Rafe, damn him, looked well rested. "You haven't missed much," he said with a tiny grin. "We were just discussing the snow."

"I bet you were," I said, arching an ironic eyebrow at him. He returned the expression with a smirk. I found myself wishing he didn't look so adorable when he did that.

Dr. Raymond cleared his throat. "As I was saying to Rafe," he said, "we have a crisis of global proportions on our hands. And it seems only fair that since you two were involved in causing it, you should be involved in solving it."

I felt as if I'd just gotten my wrist slapped. "So this is a punishment, then?" I asked, as my eyes narrowed.

The professor met my gaze. "Punishment is a loaded word. I'd rather call it restitution."

"Because that's so much less loaded," I said. I didn't mean to be a jerk about it, but come on. "Since we're making restitution, maybe we should get Hilary in on this, too. Since it was her kappa who released all the water before we told him to do it."

Dr. Raymond opened his mouth to say something, but Rafe held up a hand. "Actually, that's a pretty good idea," he said. "Can you call her?"

"Right now? I don't know if she's in class."

"Classes won't resume for another week," said Dr. Raymond. "Maintenance is still clearing away the snow."

"Where are they dumping it?" I asked as I dug out my phone.

"Boulder Creek."

"Spectacular," I muttered. "Let me text her. I didn't notice whether she was at the house today, or whether she's still at my parents' house." After the debacle down under, Hilary had accepted my parents' invitation to stay at our house until classes resumed. She reasoned – probably correctly – that Colorado would dig out from under ten feet of snow quicker than North Carolina would.

Hilary responded instantly. She was back, after all, and had been asleep until Kerry slammed her door. *I'll be there in ten minutes,* she texted. I relayed the message to Rafe and Dr. Raymond. Then I sat back and only half-listened to the two of them chat like best buddies while I mulled over the scene with Kerry. I still couldn't figure out why she had been so upset, and I promised myself that I would check in on her as soon as I got back to the house.

Dr. Raymond was the reason Rafe was in Boulder at all. Rafe had asked his brother Paul for advice on a research project he wanted to undertake, and Paul had shuffled him off to Dr. Raymond, who happened to be a colleague and former classmate – not to mention three thousand miles away.

Hilary was as good as her word. Ten minutes after her last text, she knocked on the door of Dr. Raymond's office. In the meantime, Rafe had scrounged a guest chair from an adjoining office and wedged it into the space between my chair, a short bookcase, and the door. Hilary squeezed her way in and made herself at home.

Once introductions had been made, Dr. Raymond told Hilary what the meeting was about. Her eyes grew round and her hand flew to her mouth. "Oh! Oh, no! I am *so sorry* for all the trouble Enkou has caused," she said.

"We're not here to place blame," Rafe said gently. He sounded an awful lot like Darrell had the night before. I gave him a sharp look, but he didn't see it – his attention was on Hilary, who was now near to tears. "We just need to solve the problem."

"Call it restitution," I said.

My tone must have been more pointed than I thought, because Rafe glared at me. But Hilary, still mired in dismay, missed our exchange. "Of course. I'll do anything I can to make it right."

Dr. Raymond nodded briskly. "All right, then. Welcome to the team, Hilary. Now, I'm ready to entertain solutions." He glanced at each one of us in turn.

When he got to me, I sighed. "Oh, all right. I'll be the one to say it. The easiest way to solve the problem is to put the water back where we found it."

Hilary stared at me. "You mean the reservoir in Nav?"

"That's exactly what I mean." I sat back. "The question is how to get it there. Vasily set up the siphon system to start with, and as far as I know, he's the only one who knew how it was done."

"And he's dead," Rafe said. Vasily had been the first human to be transformed by an iceworm, although his transformation had been accidental. The gods had destroyed him before Rafe's father committed suicide.

"Maybe Veles knows," Hilary suggested. "He gave the okay for the tank."

"He might," I said. "But how do we contact Him?" I glanced at Rafe. "I suppose we could do the same thing we did the last time." Which was to contact Paul, who was allied with the Slavic thunder god Perun, and ask Perun to track down Veles. The two were old antagonists.

Rafe's curled lip indicated pretty clearly his opinion of that idea. "What if we asked Thor instead?" he suggested. "He seemed to know Him."

This time, my own lip curled. "That means involving my parents. There must be some other way. Maybe Kerry could ask Epona. Or we could ask Brighid – isn't She supposed to be checking in on you?"

Rafe shook his head. "Not for another few days."

"This is ridiculous," I said. "With all of the connections we have, you'd think one of us would have an in with the gods that doesn't require calling a relative."

"I…" Hilary cleared her throat. "I might be able to do it."

I tried not to sound scornful. "You're suggesting that we send Enkou?"

"No," she said. "Benzaiten."

I was speechless.

"You've lost me," said Dr. Raymond, whose specialty was chemistry, not comparative religion.

"Wait a minute," I said. "You get *two* gods? How does *that* work?" *Hilary gets two gods and all I get is stupid laser eyes. Life is just so unfair.*

She swung around in her chair to face me and threw up her hands. "I don't know, Sage. I wish I could explain it, but I can't. Benzaiten came to me while I was at your house last week. I swear I've never spoken to Her before."

"Who is Benzaiten?" demanded Dr. Raymond.

Rafe grinned. "She is one of Japan's Seven Lucky Gods," he said. "Scholars used to think She was a manifestation of the Hindu goddess Sarasvati, but the Second Coming sorted all that out. Now we know that She's definitely Her own…goddess."

"She's the goddess of all that flows," Hilary said, with a smile like sunlight for Rafe. "Music, eloquent speech, and water."

"And dragons," said Rafe. "Like Veles. That's a brilliant idea, Hilary."

She glowed. I felt like growling at them both, but my urge didn't last long. A musical phrase, played on some stringed instrument, wafted into the closed room on a breath of sea air, and soft hands touched my shoulder and Hilary's. Hilary turned upon her goddess a glad smile.

I must have been scowling, for Benzaiten laughed at me and cupped my chin in Her hand. "Sage," She chided with a voice like a song. "Do not be jealous. Your turn will come."

I wanted to ask Her to elaborate, but She had already turned away from me. She was beautiful, of course, in a silk kimono patterned with lucky dragons, Her long hair cascading down Her back. Flowing easily between our chairs in the cramped office, She eased herself, cross-legged, to the floor between Hilary and Rafe, as if the cheap carpet were a giant lotus blossom. "What would you have Me do?" She asked.

Hilary explained – in halting sentences at first, then more smoothly as she saw that the goddess would not turn away from her. When she finished, Benzaiten laughed again.

"I would be happy to assist," She said. "I do not know Veles well, but I am acquainted with Him. And I have a way with dragons." She actually winked at us. "I will be right back." And She faded out.

After a moment of silence, Dr. Raymond cleared his throat. "Well," he said, and paused. Then he dropped his head and peered up at us over the top of his glasses. "You have me at a disadvantage. I have never seen a god in person until now. But I suppose this is a common occurrence for the three of you."

"More or less," I said.

Chapter 3

We decided the best thing to do, while we waited for Benzaiten to have Her way with Veles, was to track down Enkou.

The three of us left Dr. Raymond's office together, but Hilary moved remarkably fast. By the time Rafe and I got to the front doors of Cristol, she was gone. We had no chance of spotting her – the snow piled on either side of the sidewalks was just too high. And while we knew the creek was north of us, we didn't know exactly where Enkou usually hunkered down.

"We'll never find her," I said.

But then we heard her calling the kappa: "Enkou-san! Enkou-san!"

Rafe turned his head toward the sound. "She's this way," he said, and shifted.

"Why didn't I think of that?" I muttered, and followed suit.

I cruised along behind my Raven companion, my firebird form trailing smoke and the occasional stray flame. The walls shading the sidewalks were so tall that it was difficult to get a clear view. *Can you see her?* I sent to him.

No, it's hopeless. The snow is too high. I'm going to head for the creek. Maybe I can spot him.

Good idea.

You keep searching the paths, though, in case she slips and falls.

That thought hadn't even occurred to me. But of course, it was a danger – the sidewalks weren't completely cleared of snow and there could be icy patches underneath. And Hilary had been in a hurry. *Got it,* I said, and began flying over her most likely routes.

I was making a pass over the final possible sidewalk when Rafe said in my head, *Found them.*

Both of them?

Yeah.

He didn't sound especially happy. I wheeled in midair and made a straight shot for the creek.

I spotted Hilary first. Her bright pink parka stood out against the snow as she dug furiously at a snowbank with both hands. Nearby, Rafe had just landed and was shifting back. As soon as he was human again, he ran to help her.

One good thing about Rafe's and my shapes – our clothes somehow went with us when we shifted. That wasn't the case with my father, and it had become a family joke. I was grateful that I didn't take after him in this one thing, at least.

I began to shift back even before I landed. "Is he in there?" I called, as soon as I had my voice back.

"Yes," said Hilary. "I think so. This is where he sleeps."

The pile of snow they were working on towered over all our heads. The maintenance crews must have been dropping cleared snow from the sidewalks on top of the natural snowbank that had already been there.

"Look," I said. "It's going to take forever for you guys to tunnel in. I've got a quicker way."

Rafe glanced over my shoulder. "Oh?"

"Just stand back," I said. They complied, Hilary somewhat reluctantly. Then I turned on my internal fire and stepped into the hole they had begun. Snow melted rapidly around me, running out to the sidewalk where Rafe and Hilary stood, and down toward the frozen creek.

"You're amazing!" Hilary said.

Yeah. Sage the Amazing – that's me. "Where am I going?" I called back to her.

"Head right," she said, approaching me. "More toward the water."

"Okay, but move back 'til I've got this dug out," I told her. If it all came crashing down on top of me, I could melt my way out. Hilary couldn't.

With her directing me from a safe distance, it took me only a few minutes to burrow into the bank far enough to reach Enkou's hidey-hole. He was mostly buried under frozen mud near the edge of the creek, but a glint of the peculiar green of his shell gave his position away. "I found him," I yelled down the tunnel from my snow cave.

I couldn't see my friends, but I heard Hilary clap her gloved hands and say, "Oh, thank the gods. How is he?"

"Frozen," I said. "I'm going to try to thaw him out."

"Be careful," she called, sounding worried.

I could appreciate her fear. It was one thing to regulate my thermostat to melt a path through snow without creating an avalanche. Thawing mud without harming the living creature stuck in it was going to require several orders of magnitude more control.

"This may take a few minutes," I called, to try to keep Hilary from freaking out. Then I went to work on loosening the mud around the kappa.

I was close to being able to get a grip around the sides of his shell and start pulling on him when I heard a motor approaching. Then Rafe and Hilary started yelling. They sounded like they were both on the verge of panic, but the only word I could make out was, "No!" It didn't take a genius to figure out what was going on out there – a maintenance crew had arrived to dump more snow atop the already-towering pile on the bank. The one I was currently standing under. Which would likely collapse on top of me from the sudden additional weight.

Swiftly, I weighed my options. If I stayed, and Rafe and Hilary couldn't wave the guy off, I might be buried alive. Sure, I could melt my way out, but only if the cave-in didn't knock me unconscious. But if I left, and the tunnel collapsed, I might not find Enkou so easily a second time.

I looked at the kappa and thought, *If I give it just one more shot of juice....*

In my nervousness, I turned on my eye beams a little hotter than I might have otherwise – and saw a leg flinch out from the shell.

"Gotcha!" I cried, and put one knee down in the muck. Grabbing either side of the shell, I pulled with all my might. There was a loud sucking sound, and I found myself sprawled against the far side of my tiny cave, with my butt in a rapidly-refreezing puddle and Enkou's shell in my arms.

"You are one hell of a lot of trouble, buddy," I growled as I got to my feet.

Outside, the sound of the motor was increasing, drowning out the shouts of my friends. Then a few clods of snow dropped from the roof of the cave.

"Time to go," I said, and sprinted as fast as I could for daylight. I couldn't move all that fast — I had been going for distance rather than height when I tunneled my way in, so I had to exit bent over almost double and carrying a two-foot-wide turtle shell, to boot. But I made it with seconds to spare before the whole thing came tumbling down.

Hilary grabbed Enkou from me as Rafe pulled me into his arms.

The maintenance guy cut the motor of his forklift. "What the hell were you doing under there?" he yelled at me. "You could've been killed!"

"Getting my frisbee," I yelled back.

"You couldn't have waited 'til spring?" The guy was incredulous.

I would have been, too, in his place. "Without this frisbee," I yelled, "we might never see spring again."

"What?"

I waved him off and the three of us started for home. Four, I guess, if you count the frisbee.

"We need to get him inside as soon as possible," Hilary said.

"Question," I said. "Kappas *are* cold-blooded, right?" At her nod, I went on, "So how is Enkou going to do what we need for him to do? He'll go into hibernation as soon as he hits the first snowbank."

"There's got to be a way," she said. "Otherwise kappas wouldn't be much help to farmers in Japan. It snows there, too, you know."

Uthawahze. Damn it, I was doing it again – making fun of her accent in my head. I scolded myself mentally and, as penance, offered to carry Enkou for a little while.

But she declined my help. "He's not that heavy," she said, "and anyway, we're almost home."

I'd thought he was plenty heavy when I was dashing away from the avalanche, but I figured maybe she was used to it. Or maybe she really was that attached to the critter.

Mom always said that Dad was our pet. He could turn himself into any animal, bird, or insect we wanted him to be. That was lots of fun when we were kids. "Be a dog, Daddy! Now be a horse! Now be a panda bear!" I loved my father, of course, and the variety was something the kids in my class would probably have been envious of, if they had known. But watching Hilary cradling the kappa's shell made me wonder if *I* hadn't been the one who had missed out.

Kerry's car was gone when we got to the house. "Wonder where she went?" I said as I unlocked the front door. "It's not like we have class."

"Grocery shopping, maybe," Rafe offered.

"Maybe." I swung the door wide and motioned everybody inside.

Hilary placed Enkou on the living room floor next to the heater vent. "Anything we can do to speed things along?" I asked.

Still gazing at the shell, she shook her head. "I don't think so. I think all we can do now is wait." She took off her jacket and perched on the chair closest to Enkou.

Rafe and I traded a shrug. Then I went to change out of my sodden jeans. I thought he might follow me, but no – he stayed in the living room with Hilary, keeping watch over our amphibious friend.

Well, Hilary was keeping watch, anyway. When I emerged from my room a couple of minutes later, she was on the floor next to Enkou, rubbing his shell as if he could feel her petting him. Rafe was slouched on the far end of the couch, goofing around with his phone.

I didn't sense any tension in the room, other than Hilary's concern for Enkou, and felt myself relax for the first time since breakfast. I realized I'd been expecting…I didn't want to think about what I'd been expecting. But Benzaiten was right – I had no reason to be jealous of Hilary.

Whether She had really meant to imply that I'd get a goddess of my own someday – and whether Her prophecy would ever come true – were still up in the air.

"Anybody want tea? Coffee?" I asked, heading for the kitchen. I figured we might as well get comfortable. We were on Enkou's timetable now, and I wouldn't have put it past the irascible kappa to keep us waiting out of spite.

"Tea," Rafe said. "Thanks."

Hilary appeared not to hear me. I shrugged, put some water on to boil, and fired up the coffee maker. I thought maybe the scent would get her attention, once it started brewing.

I didn't notice the note stuck to the microwave until I went to get mugs from the adjoining cabinet:

Gone home to get my head together. Back in a few days.
Love, Kerry

"That explains that," I said with a sigh.

"What explains what?" Rafe said at my elbow, startling me so that I nearly dropped the mug I was holding.

"Gods, Rafe! I didn't even hear you come in here."

He grinned. "I'm sneaky."

"No way," I said with heavy sarcasm, shoving the mug into his hand. "Just for that, you can get your own tea."

He clutched the mug reflexively as he read the note from Kerry over my shoulder. "What's this all about?" he asked.

"No clue. I asked her about Stoner Boy this morning, and she went off on me like a fireworks display." I filled a second mug with coffee and doctored it to suit. "At least she apologized for talking to Webb when she did. She nearly got us killed, you know."

He flipped off the burner under the boiling water and poured it over the tea bag in his mug. Then he leaned back against the counter, waiting for it to steep. "You can't blame her for that."

"Sure, I can." I leaned against the counter in front of the coffee maker. "I've been after her for years to come clean with him. Why the hell she decided to do it when we most needed him…" I shook my head and sipped from my mug.

"Have you two talked about it?"

"When would we have had time?"

"Don't get mad," he said with a conciliatory smile, as he dunked his tea bag in his mug. "I'm just asking."

I sighed and took another sip of coffee. "I know. Sorry. I shouldn't take it out on you. I promised myself that I'd talk to her when I got back from our meeting this morning. And now she's not even here. So much for that." I crumpled the note and dumped it in the trash.

I must have thrown it with more force than I intended. When I looked at Rafe, he was regarding me with a serious expression. "Seems like you've been mad a lot lately," he said.

I raised my mug as if to toast his words. "It's the power that won't quit."

"Maybe you need a peace goddess," he said, his eyes laughing over the rim of his mug.

I snorted. Somehow, I couldn't see myself in an alliance with some namby-pamby feel-good goddess who just wanted to make nice with everybody.

"I wonder if Webb would blame her," he said.

"Unlikely," I said in disgust. "He probably still thinks she walks on water."

"He's a nice guy," Hilary said – the first words she'd spoken since our arrival.

I turned around to look at her. Her eyes were still on Enkou. "What?" I said.

"Your brother. He's a nice guy. We had a long talk while we were in Nav."

I considered this statement for a moment. Then I decided that I didn't want any details about whatever Webb and Hilary had discussed. Instead, I asked, "You want some coffee?"

She pulled back her long hair with one hand and flashed me a smile. "No, that's okay. But could you get me a glass of water? I think Enkou's coming around."

I think I set a land speed record for filling a big plastic tumbler. "Thanks," she said when I handed it to her, and set it down on the floor next to Enkou. A few moments later, he emerged from his shell.

As soon as the front edge of the bowl atop his head cleared his shell, Hilary upended the tumbler into the cavity. The water seemed to energize him. A moment more, and the kappa was up on his feet. Careful of the liquid load he now carried atop his skull, he bowed deeply to me. "*Domo arigatou gozaimasu,* Sage-san," he said, and followed it with another phrase I didn't understand.

"What'd he say?" I asked Hilary.

"He's thanking you for rescuing him. He says he might have been killed by the weight of the snow if you hadn't pulled him out."

Feeling a little foolish, I smiled and bowed back. "How do you say, 'you're welcome'?" I asked under my breath.

"*Dou itashi mashite,*" she said quietly. I did my best to parrot the phrase to Enkou, who bowed again. I bowed back — and then I straightened up. I had a feeling this bowing thing could go back and forth all day, if I'd let it. On one hand, that had a fair bit of comic potential. But alas, we had a planet to save. *No jokes for you, Amazing Sage…*

"Now that he's up and about," I said to Hilary, "why don't you fill him in?"

"Right," she said, and did, while I went back to the kitchen to refill my mug. The exchange didn't take long, and at the end of it, the kappa was nodding like he got it.

"*Hai, hai, hai,*" he said. Then he bowed to each of us in turn, and headed for the front door. The doorknob stymied him for a second, but Hilary turned it for him. Then he was gone.

"So?" Rafe asked as she shut the door.

She shrugged. "He seems to think he can do it. He's going to round up a bunch of his kappa friends and get them to round up their friends, and they'll all work together to get the snowmelt routed down to Nav. Is there any coffee left?"

In the end, she got her own mug, and headed back to her room with it. Rafe and I decided to relax on the couch and watch a movie together. It's not like there was anything else we could do right that second.

Our peaceful interlude lasted about twenty minutes. Then someone knocked on the front door. Rafe and I exchanged a look. Could Enkou have succeeded so fast? On the other hand, why would he knock?

Our visitor knocked again. "I know you're in there," a muffled male voice called.

I rolled my eyes dramatically. "Oh, for gods' sake. What's *he* doing here?" I said, and shot upright to give my brother a piece of my mind.

But Webb wasn't the only person perched on our snowy porch. Behind him stood two other people. One of them was a blond-haired guy with a video camera and the ugliest coat I'd ever seen on a human being. The other one was Darrell Warren's wife, NWNN news anchor Tess Showalter.

She planted her gloved hands on her hips and glared at me. "You weren't ever going to call, were you?" she said.

"Sorry," Webb said to me, with a rueful grin. "They kidnapped me."

I didn't believe that for a minute. "I'll deal with you later," I told him. Then I turned to Tess. "You seriously came all the way from Washington, D.C., to stalk me?"

"You bet your ass I did," she said. "In fact, I'd track you to the ends of the Earth. You're sitting on the biggest story in the whole fucking *world*."

I sighed and threw open the door. "Well, come on in, I guess."

A brief interlude

See what I mean about the way Sage blames me for everything?

In my defense, I didn't have much of a choice this time. Tess knew, of course, that Captain Warren had gotten hold of Sage and had delivered her message. When Sage didn't contact her immediately, Tess and her videographer Schuyler (my sister is right about his hideous jacket – purple-and-black buffalo checks, ugh) basically got on a plane to Denver and stormed our house.

Mom pretended to be shocked that Sage was incommunicado, but in all honesty, I don't think she was even a little bit surprised. After all, it's exactly what she would have done. Mom has never done more than tolerate the media, and then only if they can help her get something she wants.

Anyway, Mom told me to ride along with Tess and Schuyler to Boulder. We figured Sage would let me in for sure, whereas if she knew it was Tess at the door, she might just pretend not to be home. So I didn't actually get kidnapped, but it wasn't all my idea, either.

Don't get me wrong, though – I was happy to go. School was still out, and I was starting to develop a serious case of cabin fever. Dad had cleared the driveway, and he and I had spent the first few days home making tunnels around our property, including one to Grandfather's yurt. Dad wanted him to come inside the house, but Grandfather insisted on staying in his own place. He said the snow was acting as an insulating layer and keeping the place toasty warm inside. He wasn't making it up, either – it was warm enough in there that we had to take off our coats. Grandfather seemed to be doing okay otherwise, so we turned around and left.

Anyway, once the tunnels were all dug out, there wasn't a lot to do outside, so Mom, Dad, and I were pretty much housebound – and getting on each other's nerves – by the time Tess showed up at our door. A trip to Boulder sounded like deliverance.

And yes, all right, I admit it – I was hoping to see Kerry. I was at that mopey, relationship-gone-sour stage where it still seems like a good idea to hang around the person who has rejected you, just so you can feel the white-hot dagger of anguish tear up your insides all over again.

Wow, that's kind of poetic.

Anyway, so Tess got her interview and I got out of the house. And while I didn't see Kerry – which, given my mopey, wounded heart, was probably for the best – I did get to see Hilary again. I'm not saying she was an adequate substitute, mind you. They're two very different women. But Hilary and I had had a good talk down in Nav, and I wasn't against spending more time with her.

And besides, I got to trick Sage into letting Tess in. And I'm always up for tricking Sage. That's what younger brothers are for, right?

I do feel a little bit bad for her, though. Things are about to get kind of sticky for her. But I swear it's not my fault.

Chapter 4

When I was little, I thought Tess looked like a pixie. It was kind of comical to see her next to her husband – Darrell's a big, broad-shouldered guy, and she's so petite, with a dark bob of hair and a tiny, slightly pointed nose. But then she would open her mouth and let loose with a few opinionated *fucks*, and you knew she was no pushover. Mom says it comes from her association with Morrigan, the Irish goddess of war. But I've always wondered whether Morrigan didn't pick Tess because she was like that to start with.

Anyway, she strode into our house and commandeered my living room. "Schuyler, you should be there, I think. Let's put them on the sofa, and I'll pull over this chair.... Hi, you're the Raven? I'm Tess Showalter." She extended a hand to Rafe, who shook it wonderingly. "Sage, can we move that lamp about two feet to the right? And Webb, could you turn on the light in the dining room? Ugh, that's a lot of glare – Schuyler, can you...?"

"Already got it covered, boss lady," the camera guy said. He'd doffed his coat, revealing an equally hideous button-down shirt underneath, and was in the process of setting up some kind of screen on a pole.

"Thanks. And quit calling me 'boss lady,' damn it," she said. Schuyler just grinned at her as he screwed the camera to his tripod. It sounded like an old argument.

Hilary chose that moment to poke her head out into the living room – drawn by the ruckus, no doubt. Her mouth formed a perfect *O* and she dashed back down the hall, but not before Tess spotted her.

"Hey!" Tess called. "Come back! I swear I don't bite."

"Too hard," said Schuyler with a chuckle.

"Shut up, Schuyler. No, really, come on back." Tess actually chased Hilary down the hallway. "Hi. Tess Showalter. And you are...?"

"Hilary. Hilary Takahashi."

I couldn't see the exchange – I was sitting on the couch next to Rafe – but I heard Tess pause. "Are you the owner of the kappa?" she asked, her voice bordering on delight.

"Nobody owns Enkou!" Hilary said, indignant.

"But you're associated with him." Another pause. "Oh my God, is he *here*? Is he in there? Schuyler!"

Rafe and I exchanged a look, and sprinted to Hilary's rescue before Schuyler could get the camera off the tripod. Hilary had her back up against her bedroom door, one hand to either side of the frame, and Tess was trying to look past her. "He's not here," Rafe called. "He's out organizing a kappa army."

Tess left off trying to get a glimpse of Hilary's room and gave Rafe a long look, as if she were trying to decide whether to believe him. Then she looked at me.

"He really isn't here," I said, nodding a little too forcefully. "Come on, Tess. Leave Hilary alone. Let's go back to the living room, and Rafe and I will tell you everything." I hooked my thumb invitingly back up the hallway.

Tess glanced back and forth at the three of us. "Okay," she finally conceded. "But if I find out later that you're holding out on me, I'm going to be really pissed at you. I'd love to get some footage of a kappa. All we could find online were grainy newsreels and cartoons." Rafe and I made way for Tess to precede us up the hallway. Hilary mouthed a thank-you to me and disappeared into her room, shutting and locking the door.

The lock seemed a little extreme. I mean, if Tess were that desperate to get hold of Hilary, she could just ask Morrigan to fetch her. But then, Hilary didn't know Tess.

We all settled into our places at last. As Schuyler clipped a tiny microphone onto Rafe's collar, I got a look at his face, and realized he was terrified. That's when I realized that I was pretty much terrified, too. In fact, all of the craziness of the past several weeks – the transformations, the flying practice, the battles with Vasily, and my narrow escape from being buried alive that afternoon – suddenly hit home, and I started to shake.

My trembling got Rafe's attention. "Sage?"

"I…" My stomach had begun to roll unpleasantly. "Um…" I didn't even have the presence of mind to excuse myself. I tripped over him in my haste to get to the bathroom.

I very nearly made it, too. Most of it went into the toilet, but there was a trail down the front of my shirt, and splatters on my jeans. I'd managed to trash not one, but two pairs of jeans that day. And this had been my last clean pair.

Weird things can set you off. I started crying before I was finished throwing up. The alternating sobs and heaves gave me the hiccups.

"Sage?" said Rafe at the bathroom door. "Oh, honey." He sat next to me on the floor, wedging himself against the tub with his knees crammed up against the vanity, and put his arm around my waist.

"Don't!" I sobbed between hiccups. "You'll get all icky."

"I don't care," he said, but began stroking my hair instead. That helped to calm me down. When I managed to stop retching, finally, he got to his knees and filled the tumbler with water at the sink, then handed it to me. I rinsed out my mouth and flushed, and he put an arm around my shoulders and pulled me against him sideways.

"Don't," I mumbled. "I'm gross."

"Shhh." We sat like that for a few minutes while I cried a little more. Then he helped me get out of my shirt without spreading the barf any farther, brought me a clean shirt and a wet washcloth, and helped me sponge the gunk off my jeans. He even started a load of laundry for me.

It was the laundry that did it. I was officially in love with him.

"Thank you," I said, trailing after him to the washing machine.

He pulled me into another hug. "To be honest," he said, "I've been waiting for you to crack. The world has been asking a lot of you."

"Of you, too," I said into his shoulder. He smelled wonderful – like snow-covered pines.

"Not as much as you," he said. "Sage the Savior." He said it lightly, but I groaned. "Hey. I didn't mean it like that. It's just a lot of responsibility to carry, but you always do it with such grace."

"Grace? Me?" I pulled away from him.

"Yes, you." He touched my nose with the tip of a forefinger, and grinned. "And then you took on all my problems, too. And Hilary's. You didn't have to go in after Enkou today."

"Yeah, I did," I said, surprised. "She wouldn't have had him out 'til spring."

"She would've found another way."

I opened my mouth to argue with him, but I realized he was right. She could have found a shovel. Or asked the maintenance guy with the backhoe to help her. Not that he would have, necessarily. But she had options. And instead of letting her do it herself, I had to be the cowboy and go in with my eyes blazing. "Maybe you're right," I conceded at last.

"Don't get me wrong," he said. "It's not necessarily a bad thing. It's part of what makes you so lovable."

That brought me up short. "Yeah?"

"Yeah."

We shared a kiss that would have turned into more, if I hadn't suddenly remembered that the anchor of NWNN's premier talk show was waiting for us in the living room. "Shit," I said, coming up for air. "Tess is still out there."

"Oh, right. Shit."

After one last embrace, and whispered promises to take up later where we'd left off, we went back out to face our doom.

While I'd been busy being sick, it turned out, Webb had stepped in and played host. He had made coffee, which I didn't even realize he knew how to do, and he'd found Kerry's emergency stash of cookies and put them out, too. I felt like an idiot, but Tess looked at me with understanding in her eyes. That's when I remembered that she and Darrell had taken on their share of supernatural bad guys in their time. I wondered whether she had ever actually thrown up, or just felt like it.

"Better?" she asked gently.

"Yeah," I said. "Thanks." Then I took a breath and said, "Let's do this."

The next half-hour passed in a blur. Tess's questions led us through the events of the past few weeks, from my first dream starring Vasily/Veles up through Rafe's brush with giant wormhood. Rafe gave a succinct explanation of why all the snow came at once – which was more than I could have done – and went on to describe what Enkou had been charged with accomplishing.

While all that was happening, Webb found the two photos of Enkou that had surfaced in the CU student newspaper and sent the links to Tess. She and Schuyler decided the one of the kappa lolling in the Dalton Trumbo Fountain was a pretty good image. "It beats a cartoon, anyhow," Schuyler said with a shrug.

The only time we were stumped was when Tess asked us how long it would take before things were back to normal. *Define normal* was the first thing that came to my lips, but I bit it back. It had been decades since Earth's climate had been normal, and everybody knew it. Instead, I said, "You mean, how long will it take Enkou and the other kappas to get the snowmelt into the holding tank?"

"No," she said. "I mean, how long will it be before climate change is no longer a danger to the planet."

Rafe and I looked at each other in surprise. I mean, we knew our work wasn't done. We hadn't even begun fleshing out the project idea that had brought Rafe to Boulder in the first place. "I don't know," he said at last. "I don't think anybody knows. We haven't had time to study how much additional damage the snow has done to our climate, if any."

"You think it has?" Tess asked.

I shrugged. "It stands to reason that there has been some effect. Whether it's transitory or more lasting, we don't know."

"And we still don't have a method for removing the greenhouse gases from our atmosphere, do we?" She was relentless.

My mouth almost ran away with me again. *Hey, we're just students!* I wanted to shout at her. *Ask somebody who does this for a living, why don't you?* But I sucked it up and said instead, "I haven't read all of the literature, by any means. But as far as I'm aware, you're correct. We do not have a long-term solution yet."

Later – after Webb, Tess, and Schuyler had packed up and gone, with a promise to let us know when our interview would air – Rafe turned to me and said, "I guess we have our marching orders, don't we?"

"Yeah," I said with a sigh. "And I guess our first order of business will be to figure out how much worse the snow has made things."

"And then," he said, "we have to find a way to fix it."

"I sure hope somebody out there has a genius idea," I said. "Because I am fresh out."

As it turned out, Tess forgot to tell us when our segment went live. I suspected it was payback for my not calling her when her husband had told me to. In any case, we found out when the congratulatory emails and messages began rolling in.

Nice job, said Mom. *Your father thought so, too.*

You two were adorable! Aunt Shannon sent.

Grandpa Drew sent us a wolf howl – the highest approbation we could ever receive from him – and Grandma sent a text that was all Xs and Os, except for a cryptic, *See you soon!*

Rafe's mom, who I had gotten into the habit of calling Auntie, left Rafe a voicemail that was nothing but cheers and applause. I guess the whole Tlingit village had seen it at once.

But the most surprising message came from Rafe's brother. *Must speak with you and Martin on a matter of urgency re your comments to NWNN,* he said.

"Oh, really?" I said, reading the email over Rafe's shoulder while we lounged in my bed the following morning. "I wonder what that's all about?"

Rafe's lip curled. "No clue." Silently, he fiddled with his phone for a minute.

"What are you doing?"

He hit a final button and looked up at me. "Forwarding the message to Martin. I'm going to let him sort it out." He wrapped an arm around my shoulders and said, "I have better things to do right now."

"I'm on board with that," I said.

Some time later, we wandered out to the kitchen for food. "I hope there's more in the fridge than just cucumbers for Enkou," I said, and stopped. "Gods, I just thought of something. I hope we'll be able to keep *getting* cucumbers for him. If the snow wiped out the whole crop...."

No reply. I turned back to see what had his attention. It was on his phone, of course. And whatever it was, he was looking at it with a smile of wonder.

I stepped toward him and slipped my arms around his waist. "Care to share with the rest of the class, Mr. Orloff?"

He started when I touched him, and stowed the phone with a guilty look. "Message from an old friend," he said.

"Anyone I know?"

"Nope," he said. He sucked in a breath and said, "That was a big surprise. I haven't heard from her in years."

He was being so cryptic that the *her* really got my attention. "Oh? What's her name?"

"Bobbie," he said. "Roberta Newsome. We grew up together."

"And?"

"Nothing," he said. "We were friends for a long time. Then we lost touch. She saw the interview and looked up my email address."

I raised an eyebrow at him.

"Come on, Sage," he said with a laugh, and wrapped his arms around me. "We were never anything but friends."

"And she just emailed you to say hello."

"That," he said, "and to let me know she's coming to Boulder. She'll be here the day after tomorrow."

"Oh," I said faintly.

"Sage," he chided, and kissed my forehead. "Seriously, we were just friends."

So he claimed. Three times in the past two minutes, in fact. But deep in his black eyes I saw that hint of wonder, as if a long-dormant hope had just woken up. "I want to meet her," I said.

"Absolutely. And I want you to meet her. I think you two will be great friends. So did you find anything to eat?"

I let him get away with changing the subject. But I couldn't shake the bad feeling I'd had ever since he had first mentioned Bobbie Newsome's name.

Chapter 5

But first, we had to deal with Dr. Raymond.

Rafe and I both woke up to the same message from him: *Meeting at the lab ASAP. Bring your friend Hilary.*

"Seems abrupt," I said as the three of us threaded our way through the snowbanks to Dr. Raymond's lab in the basement of Cristol. It was still cold – all three of us puffed clouds of steam when we exhaled.

Rafe shrugged. "He's like that sometimes. He did this to me once before this semester."

"Nice," I said. Then I looked past Rafe to our companion. "Hey, Hilary, have you heard from Enkou?"

"No," she said. "But I think the snow is disappearing."

I looked at the walls of snow surrounding us. "I think you're right. I hope the kappas aren't having any trouble getting the snowmelt into the catchment pond."

"Do we have a way to check?" Rafe asked.

"I can try to contact him," Hilary said but she sounded doubtful that it would work.

Dr. Raymond, too, wanted to know whether there was any way to monitor the kappas' progress – and he seemed to want to know pretty urgently. So Hilary agreed to call our favorite ninja turtle. She stepped away from the lab equipment and called tentatively, "Enkou-san!"

The critter materialized almost immediately, threw a fit in Japanese, shook his little fist at Hilary, and winked out.

She looked at us, embarrassed. "Please forgive him for being so rude," she said. "He's very busy."

"I'm sure," said Dr. Raymond drily. He leaned back against a lab table and crossed one ankle over the other. "But has he been able to capture the moisture from the snowmelt?"

"It sounds like it," she said, "but it also sounded like the volume of water is almost overwhelming. He said he's got every kappa in the world helping out, and it may not be enough." She was blushing, but she said matter-of-factly, "He was pretty angry that I'd called him away for even a second."

"We got that part," I said.

Rafe turned to Dr. Raymond. "Is that the only reason you asked us to come here today?"

"No, it's not." Dr. Raymond straightened and went around to the other side of the lab table. Then he planted his hands wide on the tabletop and leaned toward us. In a quiet voice, he said, "Our department has been offered a tremendous opportunity to study a brand-new proposal to mitigate climate change. The timing is exceptionally good for this project. In other words, we need to move on it right now, if we're going to do it. And I think you three would be particularly suited to studying the viability of this proposal, which is why I'm offering you the right of first refusal."

"What's the idea?" Rafe asked, as the three of us gathered around the table.

"You know that one of our problems is the melting of the glaciers." He tapped a few keys on the tablet recessed into the lab table, and a holographic image of the globe sprang up before us, with the world's glaciers receding on an animated loop. "You know, of course, that the Earth has lost about 35% of its glacier coverage over the past several decades. And you also know that glaciers have a very high albedo – that is, they are very, very good at reflecting solar radiation away from the earth and back into space. That keeps the planet cooler." I found myself nodding impatiently. This was all 100-level survey course material.

He tapped a key, and the animation changed to our current situation. "What our kappa friend has done is to effectively blanket the Northern Hemisphere with snow. As a result, our planet's albedo is the highest it's been since the last Ice Age. But it's not going to last long, because the snow is melting very quickly, particularly in the tropics. That's good for life in those zones. They've taken a beating from this odd turn of events. But in Earth's historically frigid regions" – he pointed to the poles – "it would be beneficial to encourage the snow to hang around."

Rafe nodded. "So the trick will be to keep enough of the snow from receding in the Arctic, and to send some to Antarctica, to encourage the glaciers there to re-form."

"I see two problems," I said. "It would be relatively easy to keep the snow that fell in the Arctic from melting. I mean, if atmospheric temperature has indeed dropped, it's pretty much a given unless some other force goes to work on the snow. Ocean temperatures, maybe. If the water hasn't cooled as quickly as the air, then warmer air currents will cause the snow to melt and the seas to rise correspondingly."

"So we need to know current ocean temps," Rafe said.

"I'm on it," said Hilary, pulling out her own tablet. "And I'll run some calculations to see the optimal ocean temp in order to keep the snow right where it is."

"All right, that's the first problem," said Dr. Raymond. "And the second?"

"Antarctica," I said. "The vast majority of the Earth's glaciers are there, right? Something like 90 percent? But it didn't snow there. Beefing up the glaciers in the Northern Hemisphere will be a piece of cake compared to moving the snow up north all the way to the southern end of the planet."

"How would we solve that problem?" Dr. Raymond asked, his eyes alight.

"Beats me," I said with a shrug. "Giant dump trucks aren't exactly practical."

"We could get the gods involved," Rafe said.

"The gods got us into this mess," I said. "Remember? In fact, They've been almost no help so far. I'm in favor of trying to puzzle this out ourselves before we call Them in."

He raised both palms toward me and leaned away. "Hey, it was just a suggestion."

His apology barely registered. My brain had gone running off on multiple tangents. "What if we could encourage it to snow there, though?" I said. "What would it take? Seeding the clouds and lowering the water temperature?"

"We're definitely going to have to lower the water temp in the Arctic for this to work," Hilary said, looking up from her program.

"What about in the Antarctic?" I asked.

"Let me check." She went back to tapping on her tablet.

"What if we treated the Northern Hemisphere as sort of a demonstration project?" Rafe said. "If it works here, then we can work on a way to rebuild the Antarctic glaciers."

"That makes sense," Dr. Raymond said. "Tackle the problem one step at a time."

I nodded. "Okay. So how do we lower the temps in the ocean?"

"Whatever we do, we need to do it slowly," Rafe said. "Lowering the temperature too fast would have a detrimental effect on aquatic life."

"True," I said. "We'll keep that in mind. What do you suggest?"

"If we chilled just a region of water, thermohaline circulation would do the rest," he said. "We could concentrate our efforts on the East Greenland current. Greenland has almost all of the world's glaciers that aren't in Antarctica. If we can preserve, and even re-grow, the glaciers there, it would have a measurable impact on climate change."

"What about the Alaskan current?" Dr. Raymond put in.

Rafe looked at him in surprise. "What about it?"

"Well, it's a smaller project. It makes some sense to test the theory in a smaller area first."

"But Alaska doesn't have nearly the amount of glaciation that Greenland has," Rafe argued. "We don't have a lot of time for incremental testing."

"Rafe," said Dr. Raymond. "Don't you want to preserve Alaska? Shore up the permafrost? Keep your home state from becoming a soupy bog?"

Rafe's eyes narrowed. "Who exactly proposed this project, Martin?"

Our professor reddened and shut his mouth so fast I swear I heard it pop.

"It was Paul, wasn't it?" Rafe pressed. "This is the urgent matter he needed to discuss with the two of us, isn't it?"

"All right, fine," said Dr. Raymond. "Yes. It was Paul."

Rafe threw up his hands and stalked away from us.

"What difference does it make? It's a brilliant suggestion," Dr. Raymond said, raising his voice. "It doesn't matter where it came from. Come back here, Rafe."

Rafe had just about reached the opposite wall anyway. If he'd kept going, he would have had to walk out the door. Instead, he froze. Then, still with his back to us, he slowly shook his head. "Why didn't you just tell me it was Paul's idea?" he asked.

I was no empath, but even I could figure that one out. "Because he knew you'd react like this," I said. "And then refuse to help."

"I still might," Rafe said. He leaned one hand against the wall and dropped his head.

I walked over to him and put my hands on his shoulders. "No, you won't," I said confidently. "Because it really *is* worth a try, even if your asshole of a brother did come up with the idea." I massaged his shoulders. "Come on," I said. "Don't do it for Paul. Screw Paul. Do it for the Earth." I leaned in close and whispered in his ear, "Do it for me." Then I peered around his shoulder and gave him what I hoped was a winning smile.

He gave me a sidelong look. But I knew I'd won when he began to smile in return. "If I do it for you," he said in an undertone, "what do I get in return?"

"I'll show you later," I said, waggling one eyebrow as I traced his ear with one finger.

He flinched. "Cut it out. That tickles." I cackled. He grinned, and allowed me to lead him back to the lab table.

"Okay," Dr. Raymond said as if nothing had happened. "We still need to figure out how to cool the currents."

Rafe shrugged. "Easy enough. Block sunlight to the area we want to cool. Or increase the salinity in the region through evaporation."

"Because saltier water is denser, and denser water is cooler." Dr. Raymond nodded. "Which would be quicker?"

"What if we did both?" I asked. "We could get Enkou to transfer some of his team's attention away from the snow and toward the region of ocean that we want to cool. If they put the water vapor into the air above the target area, we might get a cloud cover to develop."

"And hope it doesn't rain," Rafe said. "That would re-dilute the ocean and render our experiment useless."

Hilary cleared her throat. "I don't think Enkou can do all that," she said. "He deals with rivers, mostly. This whole thing with the snow is already pretty far outside of his comfort zone."

"We need a weather god," Rafe said. "Or somebody who can conjure up clouds on command." He looked pointedly at me.

"Oh, no," I said in dismay. It was certainly true that I could get clouds to gather, just by getting angry enough. But the whole point of earning a college degree, as far as I was concerned, was to save the planet without using any of the stuff my mother called *woo-woo*. "Science must have an answer."

"Maybe," Rafe said. "But you're right here. And I know you can do it fast." He grinned suddenly. "Come on, Sage," he wheedled. "Do it for me."

You rat bastard! How dare you turn my words back on me! I felt fire gathering behind my eyes, and very nearly let it rip. But I tamped it down at the last second. I did care for the guy, but he was doing a pretty good job of pissing me off right now.

Hilary wasn't helping. "If you can make the clouds, Sage, I'm sure Enkou can handle the evaporation part of it," she said.

I threw up my hands. "Fine. Tell me where I need to go."

Dr. Raymond pulled up his 3D map again, and the three of them identified our target off the eastern coast of Greenland while I seethed.

"All right," I said. "How am I getting there? I'm fresh out of cash for a hypersonic plane ticket, and if I charge one again, my parents are going to cancel my credit card."

Hilary was already on it, damn her. Benzaiten materialized in a cloud of tinkling strings, and smoothly assured us that She could not only transport me to the region in question, but could also talk to Enkou. Hilary heaved a big sigh of relief at that, and I didn't blame her. The kappa had already bitched her out once today, and it hadn't looked like any fun the first time.

"Are you ready?" Benzaiten said to me.

"Sure," I said. "Why the hell not." I shifted, and in a blink, we were standing in the cold on the edge of the world.

"Why do I never think to bring a coat?" I muttered, sending the goddess off into gales of laughter.

"Just shift, little firebird," She advised. "You won't feel it then."

"Yeah," I said. I knew I was being ungracious, but I was still angry about being put in this position at all. "I will in a minute. Is Enkou ready?"

She paused, listening to something only She could hear. Then She nodded and said, "You may begin."

"T-terrific." My teeth had already begun to chatter. Swiftly, I shifted and took flight, mentally reviewing the coordinates I was heading for. The location didn't need to be all that precise, but my manufactured cloud bank would have to shift so it would always be between our little patch of ocean and the sun.

There. I didn't know how I knew for sure, but I knew. I reached down inside myself and tapped into my ever-present well of anger, resentment, and frustration. It sprang to the surface immediately, surprising me a little. I hadn't realized I'd been suppressing so much, and the rapidly-dwindling rational part of my brain made a note to talk to Aunt Shannon about it.

But for now, it was exactly what I needed.

My flames glowed nearly white-hot, fueled by the emotions I'd kept too long in check. With glorious abandon, I unleashed them all at once. *IT'S NOT FAIR!* I screamed to the heavens, and the heavens complied. In moments, the sky was overcast. But not just overcast. Ominous clouds hung from horizon to horizon, blotting out the sun as effectively as if day had suddenly turned to night.

I reveled in the darkness. I was giddy, laughing maniacally as I pirouetted and looped in the rapidly chilling air. I zipped in and out of the lowering clouds, their dark, smoky essence feeding my natural rage. The clouds were so thick that they obscured my trail of fire almost as soon as I sped through them. The very atmosphere danced to my tune of misery. I was the only bright spot for miles.

And then I wasn't.

Thunder crashed overhead as lightning arced straight toward me. I wheeled out of its way just in time, and the bolt landed in the roiling ocean below.

Even in my mindless state, I knew that wasn't a good thing. But I wasn't rational enough to know how to cope effectively with it. Instead, I howled and doubled down on my anger, as if that alone would be enough to fight off the elements.

Thunder rumbled again. And again. The clouds above me lit from within, an eerie, flickering light show, as they built up for yet another assault on their antagonist. As I wheeled for another run across the sky, the bolt let loose – a thick, powerful surge of electrical energy that, if it reached its target, would stop my heart for good.

Chuckling, I waited. I intended to dodge out of the way at the very last nanosecond. I was so far gone that I thought I could play chicken with lightning.

Lucky for me, cooler heads prevailed.

A blue-black streak came out of nowhere and rammed head-on into my breast. I tumbled, squawking, and recovered my equilibrium well out of the lightning bolt's path. I was saved, yes, but now I was really pissed off. *Ruin my fun, will you? Who the hell do you think you are?* Anger boiled behind my eyes.

SAGE! the interloper yelled in my head. *What the fuck are you doing? If it rains, you'll ruin everything!*

Dimly, I realized I knew that voice. Loved it, even. Didn't want to hurt it, after all.

What the fuck *was* I doing?

As my flames guttered like a spent candle, giant hands took me under either wing and brought both my attacker and me home.

Chapter 6

I probably would have slept longer, but loud voices penetrated my dreamless sleep.

Gradually, I became aware of my surroundings. I was curled in a fetal ball in my bed at home – not the house in Boulder, but *home* home. My parents' house. Whichever god it had been who had plucked me out of the sky before I fell – that much of my adventure, I remembered – had apparently been concerned enough about me to bring me here.

I was also wearing a nightshirt that I'd left here the last time I'd been home.

I rolled over. All the stuff that had been in my jeans pockets was on the nightstand – tissues, house keys, and my phone. I picked up the phone and checked the time, and was relieved to see that it was only a few hours later than when I'd left the lab with Benzaiten. My dance among the storm clouds had seemed longer. But, I supposed, it wouldn't take long for anger to make a mess of things. And I was pretty sure that in my tantrum, I had come close to destroying everything.

The voices were still at it downstairs. I debated whether to go down and join in, or just go back to sleep. Sleep wanted to win. It dragged at me, slowing my brain and making my physical responses sluggish. And to be honest, I didn't want to face the consequences of my letting go. I was warm, safe, and comfortable here, in my childhood bed. Getting up meant taking responsibility for the results of my actions, and I wasn't sure I was strong enough to do that.

But then I picked out Rafe's voice amidst the babble. I didn't think he deserved to face my family, and whoever else was down there, without me. And besides, I owed him an apology. At least one.

With a groan, I slid the covers back and set about getting dressed.

Five minutes later, I appeared in the kitchen in my jeans, a CU sweatshirt, and flip-flops. I glanced around as the conversation stopped abruptly. Mom and Dad were there, of course, and Rafe. Grandfather sat in the rocking chair next to the fireplace. He looked much older somehow, and I hoped my actions hadn't been the cause.

The other three were gods – Perun, White Buffalo Calf Pipe Woman, and Benzaiten.

I pulled back my hair with one hand. "Hi, everybody."

Mom pulled me into her arms as if I were still a little kid. I hugged her back briefly, and then pulled away. "I love you," she said as she released me.

That made me smile. If Mom wasn't mad at me, maybe I hadn't fucked up as badly as I'd thought. "I love you, too," I said. Then I turned to everyone else and said, "Okay, tell me. How bad is it?"

Perun shrugged. "Not that bad. You and our young Trickster" – He indicated Rafe with a tilt of His head – "had a good idea."

"It was Paul's idea," Rafe said.

"But you two made it better," Perun said. "As did Hilary." Here, he nodded at Benzaiten before turning back to me. "Unfortunately, none of us realized the depths of your anger. The gods erred in that. It is one thing for a god, or an elemental being like a Thunderbird, to bear the weight of prophecy on Her shoulders. It is another thing entirely to give that burden to a child."

"I'm not a child," I began.

"But you were," White Buffalo Calf Pipe Woman put in. "When We placed the burden on you, you were. And I fear that We have done you a great disservice."

I blinked. It's not every day that a goddess apologizes to you. "It's okay," I said.

"No, it's not," Mom broke in, glaring at the goddess. "Not at all."

My eyebrows shot up. But really, I shouldn't have been surprised. The goddess had yanked Mom's life around countless times over the years. It was easy for me to forget that – I mean, it's not like I saw Her in my day-to-day life any more. But if it hadn't been for White Buffalo Calf Pipe Woman, neither Webb nor I would exist. Well, we might, but Dad might not be our father. Certainly, we wouldn't have our powers. Definitely, our lives would have been easier, or at least more normal. And yet I held no animosity toward Her. Like they used to say, it is what it is. I'd never known another life. I was mad about having to shoulder the prophecy, yeah – but angry at the goddess? It had never crossed my mind.

Clearly, though, it had crossed Mom's. More than once.

She turned back to me. "You need counseling, honey. Shannon's on her way over."

The corners of my mouth quirked up. "Pretty sure one chat isn't going to make a dent, Mom."

"But it's a start," she said.

I waved that away for a moment. "So getting back to what happened," I said.

"It rained," said Rafe, looking at me at last.

I groaned. I had hoped Perun had caught me in time, before the storm could really get going. "So we're back to square one."

"No, actually, it's worse than that," he said. "The rain made the new snow in Greenland melt faster – too fast for the kappas to keep up."

I sat down hard on the nearest chair. "So what's happening now?"

"The sea levels are rising," said Perun. He must have seen my dismay, because He added, "We believe it's only a temporary situation, Sage. You didn't do any permanent damage. We simply should not have sent you out there without a guardian." And here he shot a disgusted look at Benzaiten.

The goddess raised Her hands in a graceful shrug. "If she is not allowed to make mistakes, how is she to learn?"

"The fate of the Earth is at stake, Benzaiten," Perun growled. "We cannot afford to make any more mistakes." He turned to my parents. "She needs a guardian. Thunderbird is too elemental. She needs someone who will guide her."

"We'll keep that in mind," Mom said drily. "In my experience, the gods pick *us*, not the other way around. And no one has stepped up for Sage."

"Thanks, Mom," I said. "Now I feel even worse."

"Well, it's true. Your brother has Iktomi."

"For good or ill," said Dad. The Lakota spider god was responsible for Webb's facility with knitting and weaving – but He was a Trickster, too, just like Coyote and Raven.

Perun seemed surprised. "The gods have been of the belief that White Buffalo Calf Pipe Woman had claimed Sage," He said. "Is this not the case?"

"What? No," I said. "Not at all. No offense," I said to the goddess.

"None taken," She said. "This is a surprise to Me, too."

"It is?" Mom asked. "But then where did the gods get the idea…?" She looked at Dad, who was scratching behind one ear, and crossed her arms.

"That might have been Coyote's fault," he admitted, looking up from under his lashes at her.

"Oh, Joseph," she said, in a *tell me you don't mean that* tone of voice.

He shrugged and grinned. "Hey, it wasn't my idea."

"But you didn't try to stop Him, either." She hadn't dropped her arms yet.

"Oh, come on, Naomi. How the hell do you stop Coyote?"

Mom threw up her hands and sagged back against the sink. "You don't," she said. "Of course. After nearly twenty-five years of this, you'd think I'd know that." Then she glanced at me. "But poor Sage! No wonder she's so angry. She's been all alone, all this time."

I looked around at the compassionate faces surrounding me and quailed. "It's okay, really," I said. "I'm good. Just let me talk to Aunt Shannon and I'll be good to go."

Gods and elders exchanged doubtful looks. "We will discuss this," said Perun, and motioned to the two goddesses. All three of Them faded out together, Benzaiten blowing me a kiss before She disappeared completely. If She was trying to make me feel better, it didn't work.

"So what do we do now?" I asked Rafe, who was playing with his phone.

"What?" He looked up, startled. "Oh. Well, we should go back to campus as soon as possible. Hilary's been crunching the numbers from this last effort. We need to find out what she's come up with so we can figure out what to do next."

I nodded, feeling miserable. I had sort of hoped that after my colossal screw-up, Dr. Raymond would kick me out of the program. The fact that Rafe kept saying *we* seemed to indicate that I was going to have to keep on muddling through.

"I want Sage to stay long enough to talk to Shannon," said Mom. "She ought to be here any minute." Just then, a car door slammed outside. "And I bet that's her."

It was. Aunt Shannon let herself in the front door, said hi to everybody, gave me a monster hug, and asked Mom whether anybody was using the old cottage. When Mom said no, Aunt Shannon motioned toward the front door. "C'mon," she said to me. "Let's chat."

I followed her down the driveway, feeling a little as though I was walking to the gallows.

As soon as we got in the door, I kicked the heat on while Aunt Shannon made tea. I stood in the kitchen doorway, watching her and feeling useless – the work space was really only big enough for one person.

Aunt Shannon glanced over at me. "Okay, fill me in. When your mother called me, she wasn't the most coherent she's ever been."

I snorted. And then I told her everything. By the time I wound down, it was dark outside, and we were on our third mug of tea apiece. "It just felt so good to let it all out," I said at last.

"I bet it did. You've been holding it in for a long time."

"But it was wrong," I said. "I could have ruined everything."

"Did you?"

I inspected the level of tea in my mug and contemplated whether to get a refill.

"I'll take that as a no," she said, "but you don't want to admit it."

I looked up at her in a hurry. "It's not that I don't want to admit it," I said.

"Uh-huh."

"It's not. Really. It's just that I don't know it for a fact."

"Well, we're sitting here, having this conversation, so you couldn't have screwed up too badly," she said cheerfully, refilling my mug.

"That's a bad metric," I said, stirring more sugar into my tea.

"Maybe. What did the gods say?"

"Perun said there will be no lasting damage." I started to sniffle. "But the sea level did rise. I could have..." She handed me a tissue. Blotting my eyes, I said, "I could have killed people. A *lot* of people." I crumpled the tissue and looked up at her. "And now they want to give me a divine keeper or something."

Her eyes got really big. "What?" she said with a laugh of disbelief.

"Yeah. There was some b.s. about how the gods thought White Buffalo Calf Pipe Woman had, you know, adopted me or whatever."

"Where'd they get that idea?"

"Coyote."

She rolled her eyes. "I should have known."

I grinned. "Mom was pretty pissed off."

"No way," she said, and we shared a laugh. "But you're making this sound like a death sentence, Sage. Come on! You're going to have your very own goddess. Aren't you excited?"

"Oh, absolutely," I said, deadpan. "Because Thunderbird has worked out so well for me."

"But this is different!"

"Yeah, it's different," I said. "This is, 'Oh, Sage fucked up majorly, so somebody had better keep an eye on her.'" I picked up my spoon and hers, and held them out in one fist, bowls pointed toward the table. "'Short straw wins. Or loses, depending.'" I put the spoons down and took a slug of tea.

She gave me the same look my parents and the gods had earlier. "You know," she said, leaning back in her chair, "I think maybe your opinion is skewed a bit."

I raised an eyebrow at her.

"Gods, you look so much like your mother sometimes." She took a breath. "Anyway, what I was going to say was that for most people, when a god comes into their lives, it's a very different experience than the one your parents had."

"Yeah?"

"Yeah. It's often a partnership." She smiled – thinking of her relationship with Brighid, I supposed. "They push you to grow, of course. To become a better person than you would otherwise be. But They don't typically hijack your life for Their own ends."

"Even if the continued existence of life on Earth is at stake?" I asked. I didn't know why I was challenging her.

"And that's on White Buffalo Calf Pipe Woman," Shannon said, her expression harder than I'd ever seen it. "She and Coyote haven't dealt fairly with you kids at all. I agree with your parents on that. You kids should have had a choice, but She never gave you one."

IT'S NOT FAIR! echoed in my head. Maybe I *was* angry with the goddess, after all.

"Anyway," she said, "I suspect that whoever you get is not going to run roughshod over you the way the goddess has with you kids." She looked straight at me. "Don't get me wrong – I think the goddess loves you all. But She has always had Her own agenda."

I nodded. "I can't argue with you."

"So give the new kid a chance, okay? You might be pleasantly surprised." She patted my forearm where it lay on the table, and turned to look out the window. "Wow, it's late. Let's go see what your mom's got for us for dinner." She picked up our mugs, gave them a quick wash in the sink, and left them in the tiny drying rack. Then I flipped off the heat, and we put our coats back on and headed back to the house.

"The snow's melting fast," she said.

"Yeah," I agreed, and wondered how Enkou and his kappa army were coping.

The house smelled fabulous when we walked in. My stomach growled in pleasure, and I realized I hadn't eaten since breakfast.

"Oh, good," Mom called from the kitchen. "Dinner's ready. I was just about to send Webb over to get you."

I stopped in the living room in front of Rafe, who was hunched over his phone and tapping madly away at the keyboard. "Hey," I said, nudging his foot with mine.

"Oh! Hey, Sage." He hit a key and stowed the phone. "You're still in one piece, I see?"

I frowned, confused. "It wasn't a grilling. We just talked, that's all."

"Right, right." He stood and stretched. "So are you ready to go, then?"

"You don't want to stay for dinner?" I nodded toward the kitchen. "Mom said it's ready. It smells terrific, and I haven't eaten all day."

He looked away. "Yeah. But I kind of need to get back."

"Why? Is there something going on with the project?"

"What? No." He patted the pocket where he'd stashed his phone. "They shut down and went home hours ago. I haven't heard from Martin since before you woke up."

"Then who were you texting?" I was genuinely baffled.

He looked away again. "Remember I told you about my old friend Bobbie?"

My stomach dropped. "Oh. Yeah, I do remember. Is she in town now? I thought she wasn't coming until tomorrow."

"So did I, but she's getting in tonight. I just want to be there when she arrives, you know?" He looked like a kid at Christmas.

"Yeah, okay, I get it," I said. "But I need to eat. Don't you…?"

He was halfway to the door. "Great! Thanks for being so understanding, Sage. Tell your folks goodbye for me." He dashed out the door and slammed it behind him. He must have shifted as soon as the door was shut, because I saw a bird-shaped shadow cross the window.

Webb came down the stairs just then. "Did somebody just come in?"

"No," I said. "Rafe just left." I crossed my arms and looked back toward the window, as if that would bring him back.

"Where's he going?"

I followed Webb toward the kitchen. "Some old friend is coming to town. She saw him on the NWNN interview and got hold of him. He's all excited about seeing her."

Webb stopped and turned to face me. "What's her name?"

"Bobbie, I think."

"Uh-oh," he said.

My stomach dropped again, and not from hunger. "Why 'uh-oh'?"

He glanced over his shoulder toward the kitchen, and then wrapped one arm around my shoulders and pulled me back into the living room. I hadn't realized until just then how tall my so-called little brother had been getting. My shoulder now fit under his armpit – and I am not short. "What are you, a mutant? When did you get so tall?"

He rolled his eyes. "Yeah, yeah, the air's just fine up here. Listen." He turned to face me. "Remember when we all first got to Nav, and I was all messed up over Kerry?"

"How could I forget?"

"Right. Well, Rafe told me a story about this girl he used to know."

I remembered the incident. Kerry had just rejected him, and Webb had moped all the way from our house to the Slavic underworld. Rafe had gone ahead of me and had a talk with my brother. I hadn't been privy to the discussion, but I'd been grateful to Rafe, as it had seemed to help Webb's disposition a little bit. "Okay," I said. "What's the story?"

"Pretty much the same as mine," Webb said. "The two of them grew up together, but she was a few years older than him. When he finally got up the courage to ask her out, she laughed at him." His mouth twisted. "So not exactly the same as mine. Kerry didn't laugh at me, at least."

I patted his shoulder. "She's disappeared. Did I tell you that?"

"No," he said, looking alarmed.

"Not *disappeared* disappeared," I added quickly. "But I haven't seen her since right after we got back from Alaska. She left a note saying she was going home because she needed to do some thinking."

"And you haven't heard from her since? That's weird," he said. "You two were always inseparable."

I almost told him about our argument, but I stopped myself. He'd ask what it was about, and I still had no idea. "I should call her," was all I said – and not without a twinge of guilt. I should have called her already. Sure, I'd been crazy busy, but still. "Anyway, so what happened with this Bobbie?"

Webb shrugged. "That's all he told me – that she was a class-A bitch to him and they lost touch after that."

And now that Rafe had been on TV, she had turned up, out of the blue. "Maybe she's just using the opportunity to get back in touch," I said, but I didn't believe it any more than my brother did. "Shit."

"Yeah. Let's go eat." He started toward the kitchen door. "And then I'll help you track her down."

Chapter 7

I forgot until after dinner that I'd gotten to Mom and Dad's house via god power and didn't have my car. Mom talked me into staying the weekend – "to rest up a little more" – and then Dad would drive me back to campus Monday morning on his way to the construction site in Loveland. I didn't take much convincing. The thought of taking a weekend off from all the craziness of the past few weeks was incredibly enticing.

But bright and early Saturday morning, I awoke to a text from Dr. Raymond: *Team meeting, my office, ASAP*. I sighed, sat up, and texted back that *ASAP* for me was going to be at least an hour and a half.

On my way to the bathroom for a shower, I pounded on Webb's door. Dad, I knew, would already be gone to work – he usually left before it got light.

"Whut?" my brother mumbled, his voice muzzy with sleep.

"If you drive me back to Boulder this morning, I'll buy you beer," I called. I kept my voice down, in case Mom was nearby.

A second and a half later, Webb pulled open his bedroom door. Again, I was struck by his height – and the width of his shoulders. "Are you going out for football?" I blurted.

He rolled his eyes. "I thought you weren't going back 'til Monday."

I waved my phone at him. "Emergency meeting of the project team."

He squinted while he considered my proposal. "Is Kerry there?"

I opened my mouth. Closed it. Finally, I said, "What's the right answer here?"

"Well, the right answer would be 'no,' but you couldn't tell me anyway, could you? You haven't been there since yesterday morning." He sighed and scrubbed at the top of his head with one hand, then ran the hand down over his face. "Okay. One case if she's not there. *Two* cases if she *is* there."

"Deal." We did the pinky-swear thing, and he closed his door to get dressed while I continued on to the bathroom.

Forty-five minutes later, we hit the road, fortified with a good breakfast and multiple admonitions from Mom about being careful on the road. "Jesus," Webb complained. "It's like she thinks I'm three."

"If you were three, you wouldn't be driving." I looked closely at his neck. "Are you *shaving* now?"

"Shut up," he said, rubbing his chin self-consciously. Dad's Native American genetics meant he never needed to shave. Webb hadn't, either, up to now.

"I just noticed it, that's all." I settled back. "It's not weird or anything. Most guys do. It's just weird in our family."

"Everything's weirder in our family," he said.

I sighed and looked out the window. "You got that right."

We were in luck – or rather, my wallet was. Kerry hadn't yet returned. Hilary was finishing her breakfast when we walked through the door. "Hi, y'all," she chirped. "I was just getting ready to leave. Do y'all want breakfast?"

"Nope, we ate at home," Webb told her. "I'll just hold down the fort 'til y'all get back."

Y'all? I stared at him. "I'm sorry. What did you just say?"

"I said I'd hold down the fort until you got back." He plopped onto the couch and grabbed the remote. "Got any chips?"

"No," I said. "C'mon, Hilary. The sight of Younger Brother in his native habitat is more than I can take this early in the morning."

"Bye, Webb," she called as she closed the door. Then she turned to me, all smiles. "Y'all are so cute together. Why are you always mean to him?"

"Because he's my little brother," I said, as if the answer was obvious. "Don't you have any siblings?"

"Nope," she said. "It's just my parents and me."

"And Enkou."

She flashed me a smile. "And Enkou. Hey, I can see over the snow!"

She was right – the tops of the drifts were just below her eye level. I could see clear across campus now, all the way to the front of Cristol, where Dr. Raymond's office was. So I had a perfect view of Rafe kissing a curly-haired woman on the steps before ducking inside. It wasn't just a peck on the cheek, either. They were really going at it.

My stomach did several flips before landing somewhere near my feet.

As the woman turned away from the building, she looked around as if searching for something. When her eyes lit on me, I swear to all the gods, she gave me a horrible, mocking grin. Then she skipped down the steps and was gone.

"Sage?" Hilary said. "Are you okay?"

"No. I don't know." I shook my head. Maybe I only thought I saw it. I mean, I definitely saw the liplock, but maybe I misinterpreted what had happened afterward. "Why?"

"Well, you just stopped." Hilary eyed me with concern.

I started walking again. "Shit. I'm sorry. We'd better hurry – Rafe is already there."

"He is? How do you know?"

I glanced over at her, and shortened my stride so she wouldn't have to jog to keep up with me. "You didn't see him go in just now?"

"No." She shook her head. "But maybe I missed him."

Or maybe weird shit is happening. I forced myself to smile and say, "I thought it was him, but maybe it was somebody else," and let it drop.

Rafe had, in fact, beaten us to the professor's office. He and Dr. Raymond were deep in a discussion of the data from yesterday's botched project when Hilary and I let ourselves in. "Ah, there you are," Dr. Raymond said.

"Sorry we're late," Hilary said as we slid into our accustomed chairs.

"Not at all. We were just reviewing the data. It looks like we're no worse off today than we were yesterday," he said. I was relieved to hear it. Even though Perun had said much the same thing the day before, I'd still wanted the numbers to confirm it. "And the snow reabsorption project seems to be moving ahead as scheduled. Have you spoken with Enkou since yesterday, Hilary?"

"No," she said. "But the snow is definitely disappearing."

"I've noticed that, too," the professor said.

"And since Sage was able to create a rainstorm over Greenland yesterday, there must be some moisture recirculation," Hilary went on. I blinked. I hadn't considered the rain in such a positive light before. I'd been too busy beating myself up for creating the storm at all.

During this exchange, I'd been sneaking little glances at Rafe. He'd been silent since we entered, and was alternately staring at the data on Dr. Raymond's computer screen, his own tablet in his lap, and nothing at all.

"All right," Dr. Raymond said. "I think it's time for us to move on to Phase Two."

"Phase Two?" I asked. "I hadn't realized there was more to this project."

"There is, in a manner of speaking," said the professor. "Phase Two will be a test of Rafe's climate-change mitigation theory – the one he came here to Boulder to work on."

Rafe's head snapped up. "I don't think this is a good time, Martin."

"Nonsense. It's the perfect time. We've got the team assembled, we have some data to build on now, and classes are out for at least another week."

Data? "What data are you talking about?" I asked.

"The data from yesterday," Dr. Raymond said, pointing at Rafe and me. "On the effects of supernatural events on the atmosphere."

My eyes widened. "So the whole point of this thing has been to get me to fix the climate?"

"Well, not exactly," the professor said. "But your participation certainly makes things easier."

"Rafe?" I called, willing him to look at me. "Is this why you've worked so hard to get to know me? So I'd help you with your project?"

He finally met my eyes. "Maybe at first."

"At first," I said, nodding. "And then what? What changed?"

"You stayed with me when I was sick."

"When your father tried to kill you, you mean."

He nodded.

I swallowed. "And what about now?"

He looked away again.

I couldn't let it drop. "Does your reluctance to answer me have anything to do with the woman I saw you kissing on the steps a few minutes ago?"

His eyes flew to mine. "What?"

"Just a few minutes ago," I insisted. "You know. As you were getting ready to come in the building. I saw you with her."

He was shaking his head. "Nobody came with me today."

I knew what I'd seen, though. "Medium height? Dark, curly hair? Cute figure?"

He was still shaking his head. "No. I mean, you're describing Bobbie, but she didn't come to campus with me."

What the hell...? "How would I know what she looks like if I hadn't seen her this morning?"

"I don't know," he said, one hand out in supplication. "But you've got to believe me. She wasn't here." His eyes flicked away as he mumbled, "And I haven't kissed her."

I didn't know what to believe. But I'd heard that tone of voice from him before – he had sounded exactly the same way when he pleaded with me not to abandon him to his father and Vasily. I'd been wrong then, and my mistake had almost gotten Rafe killed. Was I wrong now?

I sat back, my thoughts whirling, while Dr. Raymond went on to explain the project's parameters. I admit I was only half-listening. But when I heard the words *pull greenhouse gases out of the sky*, I sat up in a hurry.

"Run that by me again," I said. "You want to do what?"

"Pull CO_2 out of the sky," Dr. Raymond said.

"That's what I thought you said. But that's crazy."

Rafe leaned toward me. "Why?"

I couldn't believe I had to explain it to him. "Well, for starters, because it's not practical."

"What's not practical about quicklime?" he countered. "We know it works."

He wasn't wrong. Quicklime was cheap and easy to come by. My father's construction company used it all the time in making mortar. And mixing quicklime with steam heated to 400 degrees would create calcium carbonate – chalk.

"All we'd need is water and solar power," Rafe went on. "Or power from another source that's not derived from fossil fuels."

"Okay, but we'd be producing a lot of chalk," I said. "Where would we store it?"

"That's one of the problems we need to solve," he admitted. "But at least we'd be pulling the carbon dioxide out of the atmosphere."

I nodded. "Okay. I kind of see where you're going with this. Aren't there some projects along these lines already, though?"

"Yeah, but they could use some help," Rafe said, looking at me hopefully.

That look, together with his earlier comment about using a non-fossil-fuel energy source, got my attention – and not in a good way. "What sort of clean energy source were you planning to tap for this project, Rafe?"

His eyes lit up. "You," he said.

Bingo. "So essentially, you're proposing that I magick CO_2 out of the air."

"I wouldn't put it quite that way," Dr. Raymond said with a paternal-sounding chuckle, as if he thought I was making a big deal out of nothing

The thing was, I could probably do it. I was certainly getting angry enough to fry *something*.

"What about another option?" Hilary put in. She sounded a little desperate. I guessed she didn't want me to go off the way I had over Greenland.

Dr. Raymond turned his attention to her with an effort. "What sort of option?"

"Well...." I could almost see the wheels turning in her head. "What about an organic-based carbon sink?"

I liked that idea. Mainly because it didn't involve me setting fire to anything. "That's not bad," I said encouragingly. "Aren't there some grassland projects that are showing promise?"

But Rafe shook his head. "They don't convert enough CO_2 to make a dent. We'd need vast swathes of grass, and we don't have that much room any more. Not with people from the coasts moving inland to escape the rising seas."

"Okay, not grass, then," I said, still grabbing at straws. "What about some kind of fast-growing plant? Not a tree – they take too long to grow. But something nearly as tall. Like bamboo, maybe."

"Or ayalendo?" Rafe challenged.

Damn it, the guy knew too much. Ayalendo had been promoted briefly as a solution to world hunger. It grew anywhere and everywhere, and it produced a tasty grain that provided a complete protein. Unfortunately, it grew anywhere and everywhere – it couldn't be controlled. And when sprayed with common herbicides, it had a tendency to blow up. Mom, Dad, Webb, and I had helped to eradicate several fields of the stuff when I was a kid.

Dr. Raymond shook his head. "We've been down that road, Sage, as Rafe has said. No, I think his idea has real promise. All we need is a place big enough to sequester the CO_2. And the power source."

"Yeah, well, good luck," I said, and stood. "I'm not interested in being your internal combustion engine." And I left.

I had only gone a few yards down the hall when I heard Rafe pelting after me. "Sage!" Rafe yelled. I thought about breaking into a run myself, but I knew that I'd only be putting off the inevitable. Clearly, we were going to have to have this conversation, and it might as well be now. So I stopped and turned to face him, waiting for him to catch up.

To his credit, he didn't try to touch me. He must have sensed that it would set me off. Instead, he came to a halt and stood still for a moment, staring at the floor, with about a foot of space between us. And when he spoke, the first thing out of his mouth was an apology.

"Look," he said. "I'm sorry. I'm sorry I was such an ass when I left yesterday. And I'm sorry for springing this idea on you in front of the others. I should have told you about it a long time ago, in private." He risked a glance at me. "But you've gotta admit, it's been pretty crazy lately. We haven't had a lot of time for heart-to-heart conversations."

I nodded, but maintained my silence.

"I did not..." He stopped, and began again, speaking a little faster this time. "I did not come here with the intention of using you in any way. Please, Sage. If you believe nothing else I'm saying, please believe this. I've seen the way people try to exploit you. I would never do that to you. *Will* never do it to you. And I will never ask you to prostitute your talents for something you don't believe in wholeheartedly. So if you don't think my plan will work..."

"Oh, it'll work," I said.

Hope dawned in his eyes. "You really think so?"

Damn him anyway. I'd had a whole head of steam going, thinking he was an asshole. And now, here he was, apologizing, and looking adorable doing it, and offering me a chance to save the planet like I was supposed to.

If only I didn't have to *burn* anything.

"Yeah," I said. "It'll work. The question is —"

"Whether you want to do it," he finished.

"Yeah." I sagged against the nearest wall. "Your idea is viable, and I do want to help. It's just that...I don't know. The laser eyes, and the flying and all of that – it just seems too easy." I shrugged helplessly. "Like I'm cheating. Like I'm not working hard enough when I use them."

"So you make things extra hard with your self-flagellation routine," he said, but there was no bitterness in his tone. Like any good scientist, he was simply stating what he had observed.

I sighed and tilted my head back until it rested against the wall. "Maybe you're right. Maybe I should just quit fighting it and accept the inevitable."

"It's not like you wouldn't be using science at all," he said reasonably. "We'll still need to do a ton of calculations. And we'll need to calibrate your ability, so that we don't have a disaster."

"So we don't have *another* disaster, you mean. And see, that's another thing." I straightened my neck so I could look him in the eye. "I haven't exactly been succeeding beyond expectations lately. What if I screw this up, too?"

"You won't," he said confidently. "Because this time, I'm not leaving your side."

I couldn't have kept from smiling if I'd wanted to. "All right," I said. "I guess I'm in."

As we walked back to Dr. Raymond's office, he said, "So...can I push my luck?"

I looked at him sidelong. "Maybe."

He took a breath. "I'm meeting Bobbie for dinner tonight. Will you come, too?"

"A threesome? Sounds awkward," I said.

"No, it'll be fine," he said. "I wasn't kidding when I said I wanted the two of you to meet. I really do think you'll like her."

I weighed the phrasing of my next comment. Finally, I said, "Webb told me you had a thing for her."

He had the grace to look embarrassed. "Yeah, I did. But we were both much younger then. Things are different now." He gave me a tentative smile.

Damn him. I would have handed him my heart for that smile, and all he wanted was for me to meet some girl he used to know. "Okay," I said. "But can I ask Hilary and Webb to come, too? It'll seem less weird with five of us."

"Okay, if you say so." His tone was doubtful, but I was satisfied.

And I didn't want to tell him the real reason I was bringing reinforcements: If Mystery Girl tried anything on me, I wanted to have witnesses.

While Sage was out

...I decided to do a little internet sleuthing on Roberta Newsome. And I got my info, all right. But it wasn't what I found that troubled me – it was what I didn't find.

Have I mentioned that I'm pretty good at making webs? I have, right? Well, that extends to things like internet searches. I'm really good (if I do say so myself) at finding the best starting place for an inquiry, and following the thread along to its inevitable conclusion.

So that's what I did. I plugged in this girl's name and her approximate date of birth, and got a bunch of hits. By winnowing and narrowing and pulling the threads of my inquiry ever tighter, I was beginning to create a pretty good picture of who Rafe's friend was.

The odd thing was that all mentions of her stopped about two years earlier. It was like she had dropped off the face of the Earth. One minute she existed, and the next – poof! Gone.

It was very strange. And I didn't appreciate that. My week had already been strange enough.

So I opened a fresh browser page and went at it again, but by a slightly less straightforward path. I got slightly different information this time, but the ultimate result was the same. Two years before, Roberta Newsome had ceased to exist.

So I started looking for reasons why someone's online identity would be expunged. Enters the Witness Protection Program, check. Becomes a spy, check. Goes to work for Captain Warren's shadowy quasi-government agency, check.

I suppose I could have asked Captain Warren whether he had a Roberta Newsome on his payroll, but I was pretty sure she wasn't. And I was also pretty sure I'd be wasting my time, because he wouldn't be able to tell me either way.

I had one more thing to try – and that's when I hit pay dirt. And then I closed the browser, because what I'd learned was just too weird. It was so weird, in fact, that I decided that I needed to confirm it before I shared it with Sage. So I made a mental note to talk to her about it when she got home.

And then I started playing a video game and forgot.

But don't worry. She's going to find out what I discovered before too much longer, anyway.

Chapter 8

As Hilary and I turned on the street to our house, I noticed three things. First, Kerry's car wasn't in the driveway, which meant she still hadn't come back. Second, Webb's car was still parked out front, which meant he was still here, which also confirmed my first point.

And third, a gaggle of kids stood on the sidewalk in front of our house.

"You know any of those people?" I asked Hilary.

She scanned the faces and frowned. "No. I've never seen any of them before."

"Neither have I," I said.

But apparently, they had seen me. When we got closer to the house, one of them squealed and pointed in our direction. Suddenly, we were surrounded by chattering teenagers, asking for autographs and selfies.

I waved them off as best I could. Then one of the girls asked breathlessly, "Is Rafe here?"

That's when I realized what this was all about. "You guys saw us on NWNN, didn't you?"

"Yeah!" they chorused.

"He's hot!" one of the girls said, and the others giggled.

"Can you shift for us?" another asked.

"Yeah!" someone said. "We want to see a firebird!"

Just like that, my tolerance level was exceeded. "No," I said. "I'm not going to shift for you. Thanks for coming by." And I took Hilary firmly by the elbow and marched her up the sidewalk and into the house.

"Did you see those girls out there?" I demanded of Webb.

"What?" He had shucked his size-gajillion sneakers and was sitting on the couch, feet propped on the coffee table, while he played some awful video game. The game's soundtrack featured creepy music and an occasional blood-curdling scream.

"Could you…?"

"What?"

I stepped in front of the TV and put my hands on my hips. "Turn it down!" I yelled.

"Would you move?" he yelled. "I'm about to level up!"

I rolled my eyes and stepped out of the way. Two seconds later, glad tweedling sounds came from the TV speakers. He dialed down the sound and hit pause. "Sorry. You were saying?"

"Did you know about our sightseers?" I asked, pausing after each word.

"No," he said, getting up to look. "I was busy doing other stuff. Hey, they're kind of cute."

"Well, don't let them in," I said. "They saw Rafe and me on NWNN, and now they want a selfie with a real, live firebird." I plopped down on the couch and flung my arms wide. Then I looked up at him. "You're not going back home yet, are you?"

"Have you bought the beer yet?" he asked rhetorically, still looking out at the girls on the sidewalk.

"If you stay overnight, I'll buy you dinner, too," I said.

He stepped away from the window and eyed me suspiciously. "Why?"

"Rafe wants me to meet this old friend of his," I said. "So we're all invited to go to dinner with them tonight." I looked at Hilary, who was still standing by the door. "You, too."

Webb gave me that *I know something you don't know* look of his that always makes me want to throttle him. "Excellent," he said. "I'd like to meet her myself."

"Why? What do you know?" I demanded. "Is she important in some way?"

"Not really," he said, and I relaxed. "But some things about her don't fit. I'd like to get a read on her."

"Well, you'll get your chance tonight."

"Cool. Now go get my beer. And don't forget to call Kerry."

I glared at him. "Who do you think you are? My mother?"

Kerry's phone went to voicemail. I left her a message about how I'd just called to say hi, and to see if we couldn't talk through whatever was bothering her. Told her I missed her. That sort of thing.

And I decided that if I hadn't received a response by the time we got back from dinner, I'd ping Aunt Shannon. Maybe she had some clue about what was going on. I kicked myself a little for not asking her when we had our long heart-to-heart the day before, but on the other hand, it was kind of understandable that it didn't come up. We'd had plenty of other stuff to talk about.

By then, the gaggle of kids on the sidewalk had dispersed. So I went out on the beer run for Webb, and got back with just enough time to jump in the shower before dinner. I don't usually take more than one shower a day – for one thing, Colorado had been under water use restrictions for as long as I could remember – but in this case, I felt justified in making an exception. I didn't want any flop sweat left over from earlier in the day to mar the perfect image I meant to present to this girl from Rafe's past.

I really missed Kerry when I was getting ready, as I was in the habit of bouncing wardrobe decisions off of her. From what I'd seen of Hilary, I was pretty sure she'd be no help, and of course Webb was a lost cause. I ended up picking a drapey top in a pale blue that complemented my skin tone, a necklace that was only subtly Native American in its design, and jeans. I also picked out dressier shoes than my usual trail runners, and hoped I wouldn't regret not wearing boots. I usually put my hair up in a ponytail to get it out of the way, but I decided it looked better loose with that top. And then I dithered over my paltry makeup collection. I didn't usually wear any, but I decided tonight was a special occasion and daubed some on.

I must have done okay, because Webb gave me a thumbs-up as I put on my coat. "You'll knock 'em dead," he said, and then giggled to himself, as if he'd just made the funniest joke ever.

"You sure you're okay?" I asked, squinting at him.

"Never better," he said. "In fact, I expect to be the life of the party tonight." And he went off into giggles again. I wondered if he'd broken into his new stash of beer already.

I was glad I'd dressed up. Rafe had picked a nicer restaurant – not expensive, but still slightly upscale from the usual student hangouts near campus – and he'd improved on his usual attire, too. Through some kind of atmospheric kismet, he'd worn jeans, as well, and he'd put on a dress shirt in a blue that was just a couple of shades darker than mine. His eyes widened when he saw me, which was very rewarding.

Bobbie, on the other hand, was totally overdressed. She wore a curve-hugging, off-the-shoulder cocktail dress, tights, and heeled boots, all in jet black, with tons of gold chains that hung halfway to her waist. Her hair was a coppery brown, swept up to crown her with abundant curls and to reveal large, intricately-wrought earrings. Her lips and fingernails were a matching shade of fire-engine red.

She didn't look like Rafe's type at all. But who was I to judge?

Oh, and she was definitely the woman I'd seen on the steps of Cristol that morning.

"It's so nice to meet you, Sage," she purred as Rafe did the introductions. She had one of those sexy, smoky alto voices. "I've heard so much about you." She cast her eyes up at Rafe as she said it.

"I've heard a fair amount about you, too," I said smoothly in reply, and resisted the urge to look accusingly at Rafe.

Webb seemed extremely interested in her for some reason. When they shook hands, he held on overly long, and seemed intent on gazing into her eyes. I finally elbowed him so she could say hi to Hilary. Neither Hilary nor my brother had dressed up at all. Hilary had no reason to, after all – it was just dinner to her, and she seemed oblivious to the emotional undercurrents – and Webb hadn't brought anything along to change into. Not that he would have changed, necessarily. He hardly ever wore anything but cargo pants.

The waiter seated us at a round table. I was between Webb and Bobbie, and Rafe and Hilary were across from us. "So Bobbie," I began when we were settled, "are you still in school?"

She laughed. "No, I've been out of school for quite some time."

"So what do you do for a living?" I asked.

"Oh, this and that," she said. "I spend a lot of time in Juneau."

Webb's salad fork clattered to the floor. "Sorry," he mumbled, and ducked under the table to retrieve it.

"You can't take him anywhere," I said, and everyone laughed politely as Webb resumed his seat. "You should ask the waiter for a clean fork," I told him out of the corner of my mouth.

"It's fine," he said, picking up his regular fork. "I've got another one right here. See?"

I resisted the urge to sink my head in my hands. Instead, I said to Bobbie, "So I hear you and Rafe have known each other a long time."

"Oh, yes," she said. "We grew up together in Girdwood."

"Are you Tlingit, too, then?" I asked.

"Yes – on my mother's side." The waiter brought our salads, and I asked him for a clean salad fork for Webb, anyway.

"I said I don't need one," he complained.

"Yes, you do," I hissed. "Try to be classy for once in your life, would you?"

He rolled his eyes and leaned toward Hilary. "Change places with me, okay?"

"Don't do it, Hilary," I said.

All she did was shake her head and laugh at us.

As the waiter handed my brother a new fork, I turned to Bobbie and said, "I've been inside the community house in Girdwood. It's beautiful."

"Are you Raven phratry or Eagle phratry?" Webb asked. I knew immediately what he was getting at. The Tlingit had a clan system that basically split everybody into one of two phratries. In the old days, people were forbidden to marry within their own phratry – a practice which helped to strengthen the tribe's bloodlines. Rafe and his mother were Raven phratry.

"Oh, we don't follow that any more," Bobbie said with a wave of her hand.

Rafe looked at her in surprise. "Yes, we do," he said.

"Well, *I* don't follow it any more," she said, and turned to her menu. "So what's good here?"

I exchanged a glance with Rafe over her bent head. It seemed odd to me that she would be so cavalier about an important cultural taboo. And from his expression, it seemed he was stumped by her reaction, too.

The meal proceeded from there with the usual small talk. Rafe, Hilary, and I avoided talking about the specifics of our ongoing project – which didn't leave much as a topic of polite conversation except for the weather. Luckily, there was plenty there to talk about.

"How was the snow in Juneau?" Rafe asked. "Did you get socked in?"

"Oh, yes, but I dug out pretty quickly," Bobbie said.

Webb nearly choked on a bite of chicken. I patted him on the back as he coughed into his napkin. "Smaller bites, baby brother," I said sweetly.

"Shut up," he said, and swallowed. "So Bobbie, what brings you to Boulder? Rafe hasn't told us."

"Oh, he didn't?" she said, widening her eyes at him. "I'm surprised at you, Rafe. I thought you'd be shouting it from the rooftops." She turned to Webb and me with a happy smile. "Rafe and I are –"

"Enkou-san!" Hilary hissed. Sure enough, a little green hand had snaked up over the edge of the table, and was busy swiping a slice of cucumber from her plate.

"Does he want mine, too?" Webb asked, plucking cucumber pieces from the remains of his salad and slipping them under the table.

"Has he been there the whole time?" I asked, holding up the edge of the tablecloth so I could get a good view. Sure enough, the ninja turtle had leaned his shell up against Hilary's legs and was munching away on Webb's offering. I sighed and let the cloth drop back into place.

"He's not supposed to be in here at all!" Hilary said, pulling out her chair so she could scold him.

"And that has stopped him when?" Webb said with a grin.

"Who or what is Enkou?" Bobbie asked Rafe.

"He's a kappa," he said as Hilary harried the critter out of the restaurant. A few moments later, she returned, red-faced, and resumed her seat. "Sorry, everyone. I wish I knew how to stop him from sneaking in where he doesn't belong."

"You'll never be able to," Webb said. "He's a ninja." He raised his forearm to cover the lower part of his face and waggled his eyebrows, making Hilary laugh. For once, I was grateful that he was playing the clown.

As he dropped his arm again, he turned to Bobbie. "So you were saying...?"

"Yes!" she said. She put down her fork and took Rafe's hand. "We're taking a trip together."

My stomach dropped. "Oh?" was all I could manage.

"Yes," she said. "I invited him to come up and visit me in Juneau, and he's accepted. Right, honey?"

Rafe nodded silently. His expression was unreadable.

"But what about the project?" Hilary asked, confused. "I thought we were moving ahead with it right away."

"When are you leaving?" Webb asked.

"As soon as possible," Bobbie said. "Tomorrow, in fact." She shot me a venomous look.

It was then that I experienced an odd sort of optical illusion. For just a moment, instead of seeing Bobbie in her to-die-for dress, I thought I saw a sinewy brown creature sitting in her place. It was thin, with a long snout, and its arms seemed to shoot straight out from the middle of its chest. The illusion only lasted for a moment, and it left me shaken – more shaken than I'd been when Bobbie made her announcement.

"I'll be right back," I said, nearly tripping over my chair in my haste to get away. I needed some distance to process what had just happened – even if I only got as far as the parking lot.

I had reached the restaurant entrance when someone stopped me with a hand on my shoulder. I turned, thinking it might be Rafe, and fully intending to bitch him out for not coming clean with me. But it was Webb. "You saw something, didn't you?" he asked in an urgent whisper. "What was it?"

I shook my head, still disbelieving. "A weasel or something," I said. "Big and brown. And sitting in Bobbie's chair."

He nodded. "I saw it, too, right after I picked up my fork." He put both hands on my shoulders. "I think Rafe's in trouble, sis."

"We can't let him go," I said.

"I don't think we can stop her. We don't know enough yet. But we need to make some calls."

"Do you know what that thing is?"

"No. But I know who will," he said.

"Kushtaka," Auntie said, her voice so laced with dread that my stomach clenched. "A Land Otter."

We'd made our lame excuses and left the restaurant immediately. As soon as we got home, I'd contacted Rafe's mom on Skype. Webb and I had been discussing the situation with her 3D image for the past couple of minutes.

As soon as I told Auntie the name of the woman who was visiting Rafe, she had turned pale. "That can't be," she said. "Bobbie Newsome has been dead for two years."

"She died in a plane crash near Juneau, didn't she?" Webb asked.

"That's right. How did you know?"

"Yeah," I said. "How *did* you know? And why didn't you tell me?"

"Found the info on the web while you were at your meeting this morning," he said. "I didn't want to say anything to you, in case it wasn't the same woman."

"Maybe it's not," Auntie said hopefully. So I described her, and watched Auntie turn even paler. "No," she said. "That's Bobbie, all right."

"Why is she here?" I asked, nearly moaning.

"She wants to turn him into a Land Otter," Webb said. "Right, Auntie?"

"But why?" Auntie said. "Why my son? Why now? She's the one who threw him over. And that was years ago."

"It's because we did the interview," I said. "She must have seen it somehow, and decided to go after him."

"But why?" Auntie said again.

"It doesn't really matter, does it?" said Webb. "The main thing right now is to get him back. Auntie, how do you kill a kushtaka?"

I sucked in a breath. But Webb's question seemed to focus Auntie. She gave her head a little shake, and her whole demeanor changed – so much so that I could almost see the outline of Bear Mother surround her. "They hate dogs," she said. "A dog can rip a kushtaka to shreds."

"What about a wolf?" Webb asked.

Auntie looked doubtful. "The legends mention dogs," she said. "But maybe a wolf would work."

I looked at Webb. "Dad?" I asked.

"No," he said. "I think we need an expert."

"Grandpa Drew."

"Exactly."

I turned back to Auntie. "We need to go. Don't worry, Auntie. I promise we'll get him back."

"You go ahead and call your expert," she said. "I have a few things I need to check into here. I'll see you in the morning."

We ended the call, and I punched in Grandma's number. But it was Grandpa Drew who picked up.

"Now look what you've gone and done," he said. "You spoiled the surprise."

"What surprise?" I asked.

"Look out your window," he said, suppressed merriment in his voice.

Webb and I exchanged a puzzled look, and then headed for the front door. He got out the door before I did, and I nearly ran into him as he stopped dead on the porch. With my hands on his back, I peered around his shoulder.

"The cavalry has arrived," he said. And in fact, it had. For Grandma was just easing their beat-up old pickup into a spot in front of our house.

Chapter 9

"I don't know why you're surprised," Grandma said. "We told you Thursday that we'd see you soon."

The four of us were seated around the dinette set. Hilary had come out to say hi and gone back into her room. I'd made tea, and Grandma had brought homemade scones. It would all seem pretty normal to an outsider – until they listened to our conversation.

"Well, yeah," I said, "but I didn't know *soon* meant today."

"To be fair, neither did I. But your grandfather was insistent that we hit the road this morning," Grandma said, patting the stump of Grandpa Drew's right arm. He lost that arm below the elbow during the final evacuation of American troops from Vietnam.

"You drove all the way from South Dakota today?" Webb said. "That's what, eight hours?"

"It wasn't bad with two drivers," Grandma said.

Grandpa Drew blew a raspberry. "I could've done the whole drive myself, but she wouldn't let me."

"That's right, Andrew, I wouldn't. I didn't want you nodding off and driving us into some ditch."

"Now, Virginia, don't go telling these kids tall tales. You're the one who likes to drive us into the ditch."

"Once! And it was fifteen years ago!" She looked at us, offended. "He's never going to let me live that down."

"It was ten years ago," Grandpa Drew said.

"Fifteen!"

Webb and I grinned at one another. Sometimes I wondered why my mother's parents had ever bothered to get married at all. I was old enough to remember when they were still "shacking up," as Grandpa Drew called it. They were Mom's biological parents, but Grandpa Drew had left Indiana before Grandma had a chance to tell him she was pregnant. And she told Mom that her father had died in

Vietnam. Mom didn't even know she was half Lakota until all the stuff with White Buffalo Calf Pipe Woman started.

Grandpa Drew once told us the story of the first time he had seen Mom. He said she was standing outside his shack in the middle of nowhere, glowing like the sunrise, and yelling at him in Grandma's voice to open his damn door already.

"I didn't say *damn*," Mom had said.

"No, you didn't," Grandpa Drew had agreed. "You said *fucking*. I cleaned it up. I didn't want your kiddos to know that their mother swore like a sailor." And he winked at us.

"Too late for that," Dad had said, and winked at Mom.

Anyway, Mom eventually got the two of them together in the same room, and things proceeded from there. It turned out that they both still loved each other, even after all the misunderstandings, and neither one of them had ever married anybody else.

They just bickered a lot. Dad said it probably came from living so far away from civilization. There wasn't much else to do for entertainment except yell at each other.

"Anyway," I said, "it's a good thing you're here."

"I know," said Grandpa Drew. "You're having trouble with a Land Otter." He grinned at our shocked faces and tapped his temple. "See that? Webb isn't the only one who's prescient."

"No, come on," Webb said. "How did you know? Because we just figured it out tonight."

His smile vanished. "Had a dream," he said. "Night before last. Wasn't it, Virginia?"

"It was," she confirmed, and rested one hand on his arm.

"I saw a strange-looking animal seated in front of a computer terminal," he said. "And on the computer was the interview you and that young man did with NWNN, Sage. And this strange animal played it over and over again."

"What did it look like?" I asked.

"It was a skinny thing," he said. "Looked like an otter, kind of, with a long snout. But it was sitting up in a chair like a human would." He shook his head to clear the memory. "Anyway, as you might imagine, it was a little disconcerting to see this thing watching my favorite granddaughter over and over. So yesterday morning, I got Leonard going on looking into what the thing might be. He said it was probably a Land Otter, which he said is kind of like an Alaskan wendigo. Not a pleasant sort of creature, or so I gather." He looked at Grandma. "So I told your grandmother that we ought to get over here and find out what was going on."

Leonard is one of our cousins – Grandpa Drew's brother's son. He's a Wolf Dreamer, just like Grandpa Drew. Wolf Dreamers are a group of Lakota shamen who used their Wolf knowledge to help the tribe track bison, back in the days before the white man came to the Great Plains. Now they help the tribe in other ways.

"Well, we're really glad you came," Webb said. "Because it's almost definitely a Land Otter, and she's after Sage's boyfriend Rafe."

I pulled back to look at him. "I don't know that I'd..." I began.

"Oh, cut it out," Webb said. "You're in love with him. It's written all over your face whenever he's around. And he's in love with you, too."

"He is?"

Webb rolled his eyes as if the question wasn't important, and turned to Grandpa Drew. "We need to rescue him. Can you help us?"

"That's what we're here for," he said, and Grandma nodded.

The knot in my stomach – the one that had been there ever since our call with Auntie – loosened just a bit.

We were further surprised to get a call from Auntie at 6:00 a.m. She had managed to catch the last flight to Seattle from Anchorage, and flown to Denver from there on the hypersonic redeye. And she had brought a friend – a Tlingit shaman named Lawson Shakes. He seemed like a good guy, and he and Grandpa Drew bonded immediately.

"One medicine man to another," Grandma said to me, as the two men talked shop with Auntie. "How's Kerry?"

I started. In all the excitement over Grandma and Grandpa Drew's arrival, I'd forgotten my promise to myself to follow up on her. "That's a good question," I told Grandma. "She and Webb had a little bit of an argument a while back, and then she snapped at me a few days ago. Then she went home to think things over. I haven't heard from her since."

Grandma looked significantly at Webb, who was hanging onto the shamen's every word, and nodded. "He's grown into quite the young man, hasn't he?"

"Yeah, he has," I said. "It's just been since the beginning of the school year, too. It's not just physical, either – it's the way he carries himself. Like he's an adult." I snorted. "It's hard for me to think of my baby brother as a grownup."

Grandma smiled. "You think it's hard for you? I remember when *you* were in diapers. Now you're all grown up, too."

I grinned back. "Anyway," I said, "I left Kerry a voicemail yesterday and I told myself that if I didn't hear back, I'd call Aunt Shannon. Just to make sure nothing bad had happened."

"Sounds very sensible," she said. "Give Shannon my regards, would you?"

"Of course," I said, and headed off to my room.

My intentions were good, but they were derailed yet again. Because when I entered my room, I found a goddess waiting for me.

Her face was seamed and Her dark hair was shot through with gray. She wore a flowing gown of blue, about the same color as Rafe's shirt had been at dinner the night before. My heart hurt just thinking of Rafe, but I pushed the feeling away. A whole roomful of people with magical abilities were working on getting him free. I had other concerns just now.

"You're good at that," She said.

I blinked. "Good at what?"

"Compartmentalizing your feelings." She had set up shop next to my closet door, with a log fire burning merrily away beneath a giant, bubbling cauldron of some sort of fish stew. She gave the stew a stir with a paddle-like spoon. "It's a good skill to hold, as it's necessary sometimes. As long as you don't overdo it."

I should have known She would be able to read my thoughts. "Is that salmon stew?" I asked, taking a step closer to the fire.

"It is," She said with a kind smile. "And before you ask, the best of the wisdom is already out of it, gone to that lout Gwion. But betimes a bit remains." She produced a small wooden spoon from the folds of Her gown and dipped it into the pot. Then She held the spoon out to me. "Care for a taste?"

"I'm not sure," I said.

She threw back Her head and laughed heartily. "Wisdom indeed! Ah, Sage – magical child of the wise and tasty name – we are going to get along just fine."

"You're my goddess?" I asked. My eyes never left Her as I swiveled my desk chair around and sank onto it.

"I am indeed. And you know Me, of course."

"Of course. Who doesn't know Cerridwen?" I sprang to my feet again. "Um. Should I bow to You or something?"

Cerridwen laughed again. "Does your mother bow to White Buffalo Calf Pipe Woman, then?"

I snorted and dropped back onto the chair. "Hardly. Any more, she mostly seems to tell Her what to do."

"Yes, well, we won't be having any of *that*," said Cerridwen with a sidelong look at me.

"No," I said. "Of course not." I thought a moment. "But how did I end up with You? Not that I'm disappointed."

The goddess raised an ironic eyebrow.

"But I'm not Welsh," I went on. "At least, not as far as I know."

"Oh, there's a bit of Welsh on your father's side," She said, giving the pot another stir. "He's not all Ute, you know."

I had known that. Dad's father had been white, or partly white. By all accounts, the man had been an abusive drunk. Dad mentioned him only rarely, and Grandfather never did.

"Come now, Sage," Cerridwen said. "Step up. Isn't there something you would like to know?"

I grinned at Her persuasive tone. "Oh, there's lots of things I'd like to know."

"Such as?"

My smile faded. "Whether Rafe is going to be all right. Whether he loves me." I swallowed. "Whether I should use my powers to help save the Earth."

She laughed again. "You don't need a taste of this to know the answer to *that*, My dear. Why else have you been given those powers, if not to use them for good?"

"But it's like I'm cheating when I use them," I said, falling back on the answer I'd given Rafe.

"Cheating!" She seemed honestly shocked. "Why? Because other people can't do what you can?"

"No," I said. "Because then it's too easy."

"Well, of course it's easy," She said reasonably. "That's why it's called talent." She left off stirring the pot for a moment and looked straight at me. "Tell Me something. When you use that great brain of yours to figure something out, and the answer comes to you like that" – She snapped Her fingers – "is that cheating?"

"No, of course not," I said.

"Well, then. What's the difference?"

You make things extra hard with your self-flagellation routine. Rafe's words came back to me, and I winced.

"Just so," She said with a nod. "He's a wise man, your Raphael."

"*Is* he mine?" I blurted, and started to cry. "I'm sorry," I said, reaching for a tissue from the box on the nightstand. "I don't know why I'm crying."

"Here, now, lass," Cerridwen said gently, and enveloped me in a hug. "I know why you're crying. It's because the one thing neither humans nor gods can control is the heart of another."

I pulled away and drew a shaky breath. "So what can I do? He's a Raven, Cerridwen, and I'm just me. I'm so scared I'll lose him to the next shiny thing that comes along." I knew that was why I hadn't liked Bobbie. I hadn't even liked the idea of Bobbie, or of someone like her, being in his life. She was, or represented, the New Shiny Thing, and I didn't think I was shiny at all.

She stroked my hair. "I'm no love goddess, My dear. But your brother thinks Raphael cares for you. My advice is to trust in that, and see where it goes from there."

I blotted at my eyes and blew my nose. "I guess that makes sense. Thanks." I smiled up at Her.

She patted my shoulder, and then bustled back to Her cauldron. "So there's nothing else you'd like to know, then?"

I shook my head. "Other than…wait. The project." Something Dr. Raymond had said at our last meeting had been bothering me, but the world hadn't stopped veering off its axis long enough since then for me to have a good think about it. Maybe a little of Cerridwen's stew would help me make the connection. "Yes," I said. "I would like a taste, thanks."

"Good," She said. Again, She produced the wooden spoon and dipped it in the stew. My fingers were trembling so badly that I couldn't hold the spoon steady, so She brought it to my lips.

And immediately, I made the connection.

The gods had lied to us. The Earth wasn't a closed system. The World Tree tied us to other realms, other realities. And if moisture could cycle in and out of our reality, then…

Then I knew how to roll back climate change. It was going to be easy.

I turned to Cerridwen to crow about my discovery, but She was gone – and Her pot, fire, and wooden spoon had all gone with Her.

I blew out a breath. It looked like I'd be keeping my realization to myself for a little while longer. At least until Rafe came back.

Rafe! I wondered how the medicine men were getting on. I threw open my bedroom door to go and see, and nearly bowled over Grandma, who was poised to knock.

"Oh! Sorry," I said, catching her by her elbows.

"I thought I heard voices in here," she said. "Is everything all right?"

"Everything is terrific," I said. "I just met my goddess, Grandma! It's Cerridwen!"

Grandma blinked. "That's good, isn't it?"

I hugged her. "Yes, indeed. It's very good."

"Because this whole goddess thing hasn't always been good for Naomi," she went on.

"That's because White Buffalo Calf Pipe Woman isn't really in it to help Mom," I said. "Aunt Shannon says…. Oh, crap. I forgot to call Aunt Shannon again. I need to do that." I turned back to my room. Then I remembered why I'd been heading out to the living room, and spun again. "How's the search for Rafe coming?"

"Seems to be going pretty well," she said.

I grinned at her. "You have no idea, do you, Grandma?"

"All I know," she said tartly, "is that your grandfather goes into one of his trances, and comes out of it knowing things he has no business knowing. I don't know how it works."

I glanced up the hall toward the living room, where all seemed quiet. "Is that what they're doing now?"

"Yes, and they have been at it since right after you went to your room to call Shannon."

I glanced up the hall again. "Where's Webb? Did he leave?"

"No," she said. "That's the thing. I think he's gone with them."

While Sage wasn't calling Aunt Shannon

…I was trying to learn how shamen do what they do.

Lawson Shakes was a neat guy. Very grounded. I liked him better than Auntie, in some respects. She had some hard edges, which I suppose she developed from dealing with Rafe's father for all those years. Anyway, it always seemed to me that if you rubbed up against her the wrong way, you'd be bleeding out before you even realized you'd been cut.

But Lawson was cool. His sense of humor was very similar to Grandpa Drew's – and who knew there would be two guys like that in the world? They saw eye to eye on a number of other things, too, and they had a similar approach to, well, approaching the Otherworld.

Auntie had brought along a shirt that Rafe had left behind when he and Sage came back from Anchorage the last time. Lawson and Grandpa Drew both handled the shirt, getting a sense of the spirit they were looking for. Lawson knew Rafe, I guess, from back when he and Auntie lived in Girdwood. But of course Grandpa Drew had never met him – he'd only seen him on TV. He said he was going to have to rely a great deal on Lawson and Auntie for help, and they agreed.

Then Lawson opened the satchel he'd brought with him and drew out a beautifully-carved spirit mask, which he put on. Auntie had brought a similar bag which held her own spirit mask, and she put on hers now, as well. Hers depicted Bear, as she was allied with Bear Mother; his looked like an otter to me, with its short ears and long snout.

Lawson reached into his bag again and pulled out a medicine bundle, which he laid across his lap. Then, finally, he pulled out some rattles and a hand drum. He kept the drum and passed the rattles around. I took the spare. I figured, since I was sitting here, I could at least help to drum them on their way.

Lawson began to chant quietly while he beat a heartbeat rhythm on the drum. The words of the chant were like nonsense syllables to me – I know a few words of Lakota and Ute, but I don't know Tlingit at all. Still, I've got a pretty good ear, and so I picked up the words and the rhythm without too much trouble.

I remember, at one point, looking over to where Grandma was sitting quietly in the living room with a book. She had been in the kitchen before that, I thought, and had put some food in a crockpot to cook. But then Grandpa Drew yipped like a wolf, and Auntie muttered like a bear, and I got drawn into the rhythm again.

And then the rhythm was carrying me along, the words of the chant unreeling like a roadway in front of me, and I started walking. Grandpa Drew was on my right. He looked down at me and grinned as if to say, *Hey, you made it!* I smiled back at him as we kept moving.

I wasn't sure how I would know we were successful. I mean, I know Rafe, and I'd met Bobbie – or whatever you'd call the being that was calling itself Bobbie – but I had no idea how to identify their essences in the Otherworld. So I tried to let my perceptions float outward a little way, and then a little farther, and then farther still. And there, at the very maximum range of my perception, I felt a little blip.

I think I found them, I thought, and the others turned to me. I tried to point them in the right direction with my mind, if that makes any sense, but they couldn't feel what I was feeling. I had a longer range than they did, or my age helped, or something. So I went ahead a little farther, just to get a stronger fix on what I'd sensed, and waited for the others to catch up. From my new position, everybody could feel them. Lawson nodded, and Auntie's hard edges took on a very sharp shine.

Now that we had a target, we traveled quickly. We stopped just short of Rafe and the kushtaka, and Grandpa Drew and I took stock of their surroundings in the real world while Auntie and Lawson did their best to determine whether the kushtaka was dug in there, or whether she intended to move farther on. We did everything we could to make sure she didn't know we were there, and given what I'd observed of her behavior, I was pretty sure we had succeeded.

Then the chant changed slightly and reeled us back in. I opened my eyes and found myself back in the dining room at Sage and Kerry's house in Boulder.

"Was that your first spirit journey?" Lawson asked me as he took back the rattles and stowed them in his bag.

"Yeah," I said. "That was cool. Thanks for letting me come along."

"Nobody 'let you,'" he said. "When Spirit says you come, you come."

"Good job, Webster," Grandpa Drew said, and clapped me on the back.

"Yeah, Webb, good job, whatever." We all turned to see Sage hovering over us. "Did you find Rafe?"

"Yup," I said. "They're up at Bear Lake in Rocky Mountain National Park."

She closed her eyes and sighed in relief. "So we can go and get him."

Lawson chuckled. "I wish it was that easy. The kushtaka is a wily creature, and we will need to take some precautions before we're ready to approach her."

Her face fell. "But he's okay, right? Rafe is okay?"

Grandpa Drew began to stand but froze partway, wincing. "Man. I guess I sat for too long." He groaned as he stretched upright. Then he sort of shuffled over to Sage and put his good arm around her waist. "He's fine, honey. The kushtaka hasn't hurt him, and she doesn't appear to be going anywhere anytime soon. Not before morning, for sure. So let's get some dinner and talk strategy, okay?"

She wrapped her arms around him and leaned her head against his. "Okay," she sighed. "I don't mean to rush things. I just want him back."

"We all do," Auntie said, and I could almost see the whetted edge of her in her words.

Man, that's poetic. Maybe I should major in English next year.

Chapter 10

I couldn't eat that night.

It wasn't because of the food. The stew was great — although I have to admit that I was kind of shocked that Grandma had found enough real food in our kitchen to make it. It's just that I was a bundle of nerves. I wanted to be going somewhere and doing something.

I knew what we needed to do to fix the climate, but I couldn't do anything about it until Rafe was back. We knew where he was, but we couldn't go and get him because caution and preparation and reasons. I felt like a racehorse who knew the course and wanted to go already, but nobody would open the gates.

And I still had to call Aunt Shannon.

I managed three, maybe four bites of stew before I couldn't stand it any more. I pushed my bowl away and stood. "Thanks for dinner, Grandma. It was awesome. But I just remembered that I still need to call Aunt Shannon."

Webb eyed my bowl. "You're not gonna eat that?"

I made a show of handing it to him. "Go for it, baby brother."

Grandpa Drew laughed at that. "*Baby* brother? Sage, he's taller than you are!"

I smiled tightly and headed for my room.

Once the door was closed, I grabbed a pillow from my bed and bounced to a seat on the edge of the mattress. I was wound so tightly that I thought I'd better get in a few quick jabs at the pillow before I pulled up Skype, just so I wouldn't take anybody's head off.

As I was about to land my first punch, Skype chimed. *Kerry?* I bounced up off the bed and checked my tablet.

No, it wasn't Kerry. It was some kind of sympathetic magic at work. "Just thought I'd check in on you," Aunt Shannon said.

I put the call into 3D mode and turned toward her image. "I'm sorry," I began. "I've been trying to get a free minute to call you all day."

"Me? Why me?" she asked, puzzled. So I told her about Kerry being gone, and asked if she'd heard from her.

"Oh. Yes, she's fine. She's home with her parents." Aunt Shannon frowned. "She told me she'd left you a note."

"She did. But then I didn't hear from her, and I got worried."

Aunt Shannon looked as if she was going to say something, but then she stopped, and tapped her upper lip with a forefinger. "You know, Sage," she said, and paused again. "I should probably let Kerry speak for herself."

"No, go on," I said. "What were you going to say?"

"Just that Kerry isn't quite as shallow as she seems to be. She was really bothered by your reaction to her last boyfriend."

"You mean Stoner Boy?" I said with a laugh. "Let me tell you something, Aunt Shannon. If you had met him, you would have felt the same way about him."

"Probably," she admitted. "But what really got to Kerry was that you turned out to be right. She felt like he betrayed her trust."

"He did betray her trust," I said. "He betrayed everybody's trust. He had the student paper publish a photo he took in my room, without asking for anyone's permission. I'm pretty sure that's illegal in some states."

Her mouth quirked up at the corners. "I get that you have a valid complaint against him," she said. "But think about it, Sage. You've objected to every choice she's made this semester, and you've been right every time. She knew you were upset with her. So she tried to do something right by finally talking to Webb, which I gather you've been after her to do for quite a while."

"Oh, shit," I said faintly as I finally caught on. "And now I'm mad at her because her timing sucked."

"And you were right again," she said. "She nearly got you killed. And she knows that."

I closed my eyes. Kerry had said all of this to me, but I hadn't been listening. "No wonder she hasn't come back. She must feel terrible." I met Aunt Shannon's holographic eyes. "Please tell her I'm sorry. I didn't mean to act like a jerk. And I miss her and I want her to come back."

Aunt Shannon nodded. "I will. Just try not to be so judgmental around her, okay? We're all doing the best we can. Kerry, too."

"I know. Gods, I feel terrible."

She gave me an understanding smile. Then she said, "So. Have you heard from your goddess yet?"

"Oh, my gods, yes!" I said. "It's Cerridwen, and She's amazing!"

"Cerridwen, huh?" she said, grinning at my excitement. "Has She made you any wiser?"

"As a matter of fact," I said, and paused. "Aunt Shannon, how hard would it be to call a meeting of the gods? For, like, tomorrow afternoon?"

Her eyes widened. "Well, on such short notice, you wouldn't be able to get everybody there. But you'd probably get a good number of Them. Why?"

"Because I have a bone to pick with Them."

"Oh, really?" said a now-familiar voice at my elbow, as its owner leaned over my shoulder to look at Aunt Shannon's holograph. "So this is the famous Shannon McDonough? Brighid has nothing but nice things to say about you." She peered at her more closely. "I thought you would be more substantial, though."

Aunt Shannon laughed. "Hi, Cerridwen. I'm not actually there."

"Ah," She said, with a mysterious air. "Technology." She turned to me. "So what is this meeting of the gods about? Does it have anything to do with your insight this afternoon?"

"That's exactly what it's about. Can You spread the word?" The words slipped out before I thought about who I was talking to. My face grew warm as I said, "Or rather, would You please spread the word?"

She nodded regally. "Thank you for putting it so nicely." Then Her manner grew more relaxed. "I would be more than happy to help. It's about time We did something about this climate nonsense. Would you please let Brighid know, Shannon? And I will contact as many of the others as I can." She waved to the holograph as She began to fade out.

"Will do. I'll talk to you later, Sage."

"Bye, Aunt Shannon. And thank you for everything."

She grinned and ended the call.

I took a deep breath and looked around my room. It suddenly seemed too quiet, too empty, with just me in it.

There was life and light out in the living room, I knew. And it was full of people I knew and loved. But the two people I really wanted to be with were missing. One of them was Kerry, my best friend, who I'd been too hard on, even though it turned out I'd been right. And the other one was Rafe, who was in the clutches of a monster, and whose rescue party seemed content to sit around and play pinochle or something while waiting for daylight.

Maybe that wasn't fair. Planning was important, after all. But I wanted him here *now*.

I drew in a breath. At least I'd managed to get something done. Tomorrow, I was going to have a word with the gods about fixing Earth's climate – and what They were going to have to do to help.

Sage, the little firebird, was going to try to push the gods around? Maybe I was my mother's daughter, after all.

I did eventually go back out to the living room. "There you are," Grandpa Drew said as I emerged from the hallway. "For a minute, I thought we'd have to send someone in after you."

I blinked. "Why? Did I miss something?"

"Not yet," Auntie said. "But we need you to help us fight the kushtaka." She had pulled over one of the dinette chairs and placed it in front of the TV, because every other seat in the room was taken. Grandma and Grandpa Drew were on the couch, with Webb at the far end next to Grandma and Hilary squeezed in next to him. Lawson had grabbed the recliner.

I could have done the same thing as Auntie had, but the couch was closer. I perched on the arm next to Grandpa Drew and hoped the whole thing wouldn't give way. It was a freecycled couch to start with, and Kerry and I had repaired it together, with screws, glue, and a weaving job that used about a hundred feet of climbing rope.

Thinking of that day, I missed her all over again. And thinking of missing people reminded me of Rafe. "What do you want me to do?" I asked.

"Come along for the ride," Grandpa Drew said.

"What? Now?" I looked out the window reflexively. "It must be past ten o'clock."

"No, no," Lawson said. "First thing in the morning." And he went on to outline the plan.

They wanted to spook Bobbie into leaving Rafe alone. As Webb had mentioned earlier, kushtakas were afraid of dogs – probably because a dog's sharp sense of smell could sniff out a creature that wasn't what it appeared to be. We didn't have a dog, but we did have Grandpa Drew, and he'd brought his Wolf Dreamer regalia along. At first light, he was going to approach Bobbie and try to chase her off.

I was skeptical. It's not like you couldn't tell the difference between a dog and a seventy-year-old guy in a wolf costume, even if it was still mostly dark. "What's our Plan B?" I asked.

Lawson patted his satchel. "Right here," he said. He had a kind of ritual power over Land Otters, by virtue of an item in his medicine bundle that he had won from one of the creatures several decades before. If Grandpa Drew didn't succeed in scaring Bobbie away, then Lawson was prepared to perform a banishing ritual. But that could get complicated. The goal of any Land Otter was to turn some unsuspecting human into a Land Otter, too. Lawson's theory was that Bobbie had seen Rafe on TV and decided to come down here to grab him as her mate. "If she's had any success at all in turning him," Lawson said, "the banishing ritual could affect him, too."

"You mean he'd have to go with her?" I said. "We can't let that happen."

"That's why we need you," Grandpa Drew said, patting my knee. "While us old farts — and Webb here — are keeping the kushtaka busy, we need you to get Rafe out of there."

"Terrific." I wondered what sort of shiny thing I could use to attract Rafe's attention so that he'd come with me. "Auntie," I asked, "Can you think of anything that Rafe would never give up? I'm wondering what I can use as bait."

She looked at me in mild surprise. "Don't sell yourself short, my dear."

I looked down at my hands folded in my lap. Intellectually, I understood what she was telling me. It was the same thing Webb had told me, and the same thing Cerridwen had said. When I weighed the evidence logically and dispassionately, I knew that they were probably right.

But the *probably* part bothered me. None of them had been with us when Rafe was teaching me how to fly. They hadn't seen him veer off repeatedly to check out the newest shiny thing that caught his eye below. And I just wasn't convinced that I would ever be able to out-shiny Bobbie — especially if she had some kind of supernatural hold on him.

And then it hit me. There was one thing I could do that Bobbie, living or Land Otter, would never be able to do. And it was something Rafe loved more than just about anything else. Something he would never willingly give up.

I nodded. "Okay. Let's do this."

The older folks all declined my offer to stay overnight with us, opting to get hotel rooms nearby instead. But Webb stretched out on the couch and was asleep almost immediately.

"Wouldn't it be nice to fall asleep so easily?" I said to Hilary as we headed down the hall to our rooms. "Ah, to be young and innocent again."

She smirked. "Because you're such a woman of the world."

"It's true that I'm not that much older," I said as we paused at my door. "But I've always felt like I was light years ahead of him in maturity level." I glanced back up the hallway. "Until these last few weeks. I don't know what's going on, but it's almost like he's turning into an adult before my eyes."

"Guys grow up, too," she said softly, looking back toward the living room.

"That's what I hear. This is the first time I've actually seen it happen, though." I gave her a quirky smile as I opened my door. "You're coming with us in the morning?"

She nodded. "Someone has to man the command post. I guess I drew the short straw."

"It shouldn't be difficult. I think your hardest job will be keeping Grandma from falling asleep."

She giggled. "Goodnight, Sage."

"Goodnight. And Hilary?" She turned back toward me. "Thanks."

"It's a no-brainer," she said. "He's my friend, too, you know."

I was in bed and nearly asleep when I realized that I hadn't made fun of Hilary's accent for at least twenty-four hours. Maybe *I* was maturing, too.

Chapter 11

You know how it is when you know you have to get up much earlier than usual, and so you never really fall soundly asleep because you're afraid you'll sleep through the alarm? Well, that's the kind of night I had. My alarm was set for the ungodly hour of 4:30 a.m. By the time 4:20 rolled around, I had jerked awake, certain that I was oversleeping, at least half a dozen times. Finally, I gave up and went to the kitchen to start the coffee.

Webb, too, was already up. He was playing some video game with the lights off and his earbuds in. The action on the TV screen made eerie, fluttering shadows on the living room walls. I couldn't take it – I had to turn on a lamp. He turned to me, blinking against the brightness, and unplugged one ear.

"How much sleep did you get?" I asked.

"Not a lot." He stood and stretched. "What time is it?"

"Not quite 4:30. Lawson and Auntie are due here at 5:00, right?"

"Yeah." He yawned and then sniffed at his underarms. "This is day three for this shirt. Mom's going to have to burn it."

"You should have said something. I could have run a load of laundry." I flashed on the memory of Rafe helping me with the last load of laundry I'd done, and had to sit down for a minute.

"Sage?"

I drew a shaky breath. "I just hope this works, that's all."

He pulled me to my feet and gave me a hug. "It will. Somehow or other, we're going to make it work."

I looked up at him. "Is that a prophecy or a guess?"

He smiled enigmatically in reply.

I took a breath – in preparation for sighing, I guess – but coughed instead. Waving my hand in front of my face, I said, "Wow. I think Mom *will* have to burn that shirt."

It was 5:00 a.m. exactly when Lawson knocked on our door. The eastern sky had yet to begin to lighten as the three of us huddled in our jackets and filed out to the waiting cars. Hilary opted to go with Webb in Lawson and Auntie's rental. So that we wouldn't have to do the sardine thing, I went with Grandma and Grandpa Drew in their truck.

It was apparently too early for bickering, or else the gravity of the job at hand had sobered my grandparents. In any case, it was a silent hour's ride up to Estes Park. I tried not to fidget too much, even though I was pretty tightly wound. I must have been twitchier than I thought, though, because at one point Grandma patted my knee − a sort of *there, there, dear* that didn't do much of anything to calm my nerves.

Dawn was breaking as we entered the park and took the turnoff to Bear Lake. "She couldn't have picked a place a little closer to the entrance, could she?" Grandpa Drew groused as he maneuvered the old truck around the final set of switchbacks. It was the first thing any of us had said since leaving Boulder.

Ahead of us, Lawson pulled off onto the shoulder at the entrance to the Bear Lake trailhead. He got out of his car and grabbed his medicine bag from the trunk. Then he walked back to our truck. Grandpa Drew rolled down his window and asked, "What's the plan?"

"I think we should do a little reconnaissance," Lawson said. "Make sure they haven't moved since last night."

"Sounds good." Grandpa Drew opened his door and got out. "You coming, Sage?"

"Sure. Yeah." I slid out after him.

We walked single-file to the trailhead, Webb and Auntie joining us at the back of the group. I watched my breath fog the air in the pink-and-gray light. Lawson stepped off the trail and went about twenty or thirty feet into the woods, bringing us to a halt in a decent-sized clearing. He handed around some rattles from his satchel and said, "Soft and low, now. We don't want to draw attention to ourselves. We just need to make sure that she's still there." And he began the chant.

The whole thing seemed surreal to me, so I wasn't surprised when I was drawn into the vision. Grandpa Drew bounded ahead, his Wolf senses sniffing the air for any scent of our quarry. Bear Mother lumbered just behind him, intent on snatching back Her cub from the creature who had stolen him away from Her.

And then I was above them all, darting in and out of the trees with my fire banked, looking for Raven.

My airy vantage point allowed me to spot him first. Stifling my cry of success, I wheeled away and returned to the group. "He's on the far side," I told them excitedly, "in a sleeping bag about thirty yards from the lake's edge. She's asleep next to him."

"It's showtime," Grandpa Drew said, and unzipped his coat to reveal his regalia. He stowed the coat next to Lawson's bag, and kicked some leaves over both, to make them less conspicuous to any early-morning hikers. Then, alternately chanting and yipping, he began the short hike around the lake to the right. Lawson and Auntie donned their costumes and followed him.

Webb and I looked at one another. "You're coming with me, then?" I asked. At his nod, I motioned to him to follow me as I took the left-hand trail.

We were about a third of the way around the lake when the commotion started. First, we heard Grandpa Drew's howl. Then a bear roared, and there was a great deal of snarling.

"That's my cue," I said to Webb. "If he runs this way, catch him, okay?"

He pulled a wad of yarn out of his coat pocket. "I'm ready," he said.

I gave him a thumbs-up. Then I shifted and shot up through the trees.

A firebird is nothing if not conspicuous, but I banked my flames as much as I could, hoping I would look like nothing more than an exotic orange bird. In seconds, I reached the campsite where Rafe and Bobbie had spent the night. It was clearly a temporary setup — just sleeping bags and the cold remains of an obviously unauthorized campfire. Bobbie's sleeping bag was empty, but Rafe was still curled up inside his. He had cinched the hood of the bag tight around his head so that only his eyes and nose showed.

Farther off in the trees, I could hear the kushtaka's snarls, as well as a bear whuffling, and the growling of more than one wolf. I wondered briefly where the reinforcements had come from, and then remembered what I was here for.

I shifted back and knelt beside Rafe, softly calling his name.

At first, he didn't move. Then he jerked, and a moan escaped him.

"Rafe!" I hissed.

"Go away," he said, and tried to pull the hood over his head.

"Rafe!" I said again, and shook him. "Rafe, it's Sage. You need to wake up and come with me!"

Nothing.

I was on the edge of panic. "Damn it, Rafe, come on. Quit acting stupid and come on. Your mom and Lawson and Grandpa Drew have her occupied right now, but I don't know how long they can keep her distracted. You have to come *now*."

"I can't," he said, sounding lost. "You're one of them."

"No, I'm not," I said. "I'm *not* a kushtaka, Rafe. I'm Sage, and I'm alive. And you're alive. But if you don't come with me right now, you'll be stuck here forever." I swallowed and pulled out my best shiny thing. "Come now, or you'll never fly again."

At last, I had his attention. He peered out at me through the tiny opening in the bag. "Fly?"

"Yes, fly," I said, exasperated. "Now come on out of there, before I come in after you." I looked over my shoulder toward the sounds of the struggle. I couldn't tell whether they were closer or farther away, but in either case, I wanted to be gone.

"She said I couldn't fly any more."

That brought me up short. What the hell had she done to him? "Well, I say you can. Why don't you get out of that sleeping bag and we'll see who's right."

He fumbled his way out of the hood, and I helped him with the zipper. A moment more, and he stood before me, coatless in the early-morning chill, and wearing the same blue shirt he'd had on at the restaurant Saturday night. "That's gonna be another shirt for the bonfire, I bet," I muttered.

"What?"

"I'll explain later." I glanced again toward the battle. When I returned my attention to him, he was wearing me a soft, wondering smile. I frowned. "What?"

"It really is you." He reached out with one hand and stroked my cheek with his thumb. "It really is you."

Tears welled up and spilled over. "I was so scared," I said, and hugged him as tightly as I could. But after a moment, I stepped back and wiped my nose on my coat sleeve. "Let's get out of here, okay?"

He had no trouble shifting, after all. In a moment, we were both airborne. *I knew she was feeding you bullshit,* I sent to him as I led the way to the trailhead.

He cawed gleefully as we began our descent.

Grandma had already backed the truck around. "I saw you coming back in a blaze of light," she told me. "Hop in, you two." She gunned the motor as Hilary scooted over to make room for us.

"But what about the others?" I asked, looking back toward the lake. I could still hear the battle, but faintly now.

Webb was right behind us. "I'll tell them. You go on."

I motioned to the yarn he still held in his hand. "Sorry you didn't get to use that."

"I never said it was for Rafe," he said, with a Trickster grin.

"See you later, Webb," Hilary called as we piled in.

Even as thrilled as I was to have Rafe back, I couldn't help but notice the look she was giving my baby brother. My head swiveled automatically, and I noted that he wore a very similar look. *Oh, really?*

I caught his eye and made sure he saw my enigmatic smile. In return, he scowled at me. I burst into laughter and rolled the window down. "You can dish it out but you can't take it, huh?" I yelled.

"Shut up!" he yelled after me as we pulled away.

I dropped my head onto Rafe's shoulder and sighed. At least this one thing had gone right this morning, and the day was still young.

Really young.

"Shit," I said.

Grandma hit the brakes and looked at me, instantly worried. "What? What is it?"

"Oh, no," I said, sorry that I'd upset her. "It's not about this. I'm sure Grandpa Drew and the others will be fine."

She relaxed and resumed driving. "What, then?"

I swallowed. "I just remembered that I've got an appointment with the gods this afternoon."

"What?" Rafe said.

I leaned my head on his shoulder again. "Yeah. We've got a lot of catching up to do."

What happened to the kushtaka

I stood on the road for a moment, watching them drive away. My emotions were in turmoil. Yes, I wanted to throttle Sage, but that was nothing new. What confused me was Hilary.

She was awfully cute, and very sweet. She was also a brainiac, and a lot more capable than she usually let on – witness the way she managed Enkou. There was more to it than just feeding him cucumbers to keep him quiet. And he knew it. Yes, he was cranky a lot of the time, but he respected her, too.

I respected her.

But wasn't I still in love with Kerry? If I could get over her that fast, had I ever really been in love with her at all?

Questions for the ages, for sure. And I didn't have time to give them all the pondering they deserved. Back to the trailhead I went.

Every now and then, I wished for a magical power that would allow me to cover great distances in a single bound. Alas, I had to work with what the gods had granted me. So I took the trail at a run, and hoped I wouldn't be too late.

The shamen had herded the kushtaka a good distance away from her camp. I passed the cold campfire and rumpled sleeping bags several minutes before coming upon the group. They had backed her up against an overhanging ledge and stood in a semicircle around her. Lawson was chanting – an otherworldly sound – and occasionally making threatening moves toward her. Every time, she would slam herself back against the granite and hiss. Auntie was holding her own. But Grandpa Drew was clearly feeling his age. I mean, he was in good shape and all, but he was over seventy. He probably wasn't used to an early morning jog any more, let alone fighting cranky critters like this kushtaka. And the kushtaka, who had dropped all illusion of humanity and stood before them in her true form, knew he was in trouble. She kept flicking her glance toward him, as if gauging how much longer before she could overrun him.

To make matters worse, I could hear running water not far off. If she got to that creek, we would lose our opportunity to capture and subdue her – and who knew what she might do later to retaliate? No, we had to grab her now, or it was game over for Rafe – and maybe for the rest of us, too.

Several real wolves had been drawn to the battle by Grandpa Drew's presence. I could sense them lying in wait for the creature in the surrounding woods. But attacking her would only end badly for them; they didn't have the power to go head-to-head with a magical creature.

I, on the other hand, did.

Yarn in hand, I crept through the trees as soundlessly as I could, and counted on the shadows to conceal me. The day was brightening, but in this copse of trees the sun had yet to penetrate. I aimed for a spot well behind the group, between Grandpa Drew and the creek. Once there, I set up my snare, and hunkered down to wait.

I didn't have to wait long. The higher the sun rose, the greater the chance for discovery – and the kushtaka knew it. Without warning, she sprang at Grandpa Drew. The others moved to attack her, but he was down and she was already gone.

The wolves were on their feet, baying, and racing toward the creature. They must have understood what I had been up to, because they herded her toward my snare. She barked in glee – I'm sure she thought them stupid for pushing her toward the creek – and went right where they wanted her to go. The trip wire twanged, the snare shot up, and in moments it was over.

While the wolves surrounded her, making sure she wasn't going anywhere, I ran back to check on Grandpa Drew. He had regained his feet and stood now, braced against the bottom of the ledge, as he catalogued his injuries.

Lawson and Auntie left him to me while they went to dispatch the kushtaka. "Are you okay?" I asked.

"Tired," he wheezed. "And a little banged up. I think I bruised a rib when that thing knocked me down." He winced as he wrapped his good arm around his torso.

"Do you want to sit down?"

"Nah. I'd just have to get back up again. I'm fine right here." He patted my shoulder with his stump. "Glad you got here when you did, son. That snare is a nice piece of work. Worthy of a warrior."

The blood of three honorable tribes – Ute, Lakota, and Celt – ran in my veins, and all three of them sang in response to his praise. "Thanks," I said, grinning like an idiot.

A blood-curdling shriek rent the air. The wolves barked, and the birds high in the trees erupted in cries that sounded like screaming. Grandpa Drew's shoulders sagged. "It's over," he said.

"You don't sound happy," I said, my smile slowly fading.

He fixed me with a stare. "This isn't one of your video games, Webb. Some poor creature just lost her life."

"She wasn't technically alive, Grandpa Drew," I said.

But he ignored me. Clutching his sore middle, he raised his voice in a thin, mournful howl. Chills ran down my spine as one by one, the wolves joined the chorus. It went on for several minutes – long enough for his words to sink in.

I knew better than to believe in evil. I hadn't yet been born when the gods came back to Earth, so I had lived my whole life under their mostly benevolent rule. Because of that, I knew that everything that existed on Earth had its place. Humans called things "good" because we perceived them as beneficial to us – but there was a flip side to every coin, a yang for every yin. Things exist for a reason. Things happen for a reason.

We might never know the reason why the kushtaka went after Rafe. But she had lived, in her own way, and now her life was over.

At last, I bowed my head and silently asked the gods to speed the creature's passage to whatever afterlife she was destined for.

Chapter 12

I should have known it was too easy.

Rafe seemed fine for the first few miles. Then his head sank down on top of mine. That didn't worry me — I figured he hadn't gotten a whole lot of sleep for the past two nights, huddled in a sleeping bag in subzero temperatures. And I had no idea how he and Bobbie had gotten to the park. For all I knew, they had walked the forty miles.

But when Grandma pulled into our driveway, he wouldn't wake up.

Grandma and Hilary slid out on the driver's side. I opened the passenger's side door and nudged him. "Rafe, honey, we're home. Well, we're at my house," I amended. "Come on."

His head dropped back until it hit the back window of the pickup, and even that didn't rouse him.

I laughed softly. "Wow, you're out for the count. Rafe?" I shook him. "Rafe?"

Still no response. With nothing bracing him any more, he began to fall sideways toward me.

I pushed him back into a sitting position and yelled for Hilary over my shoulder. She was already on the porch, but she was back in a heartbeat. "I can't wake him up," I said. This was starting to remind me of the trouble I had at Bear Lake, when I couldn't rouse him enough to get him out of the sleeping bag. "Help me get him into the house."

She nodded. After I wrestled with him ineffectually for a minute or two — it's not easy to move a dead weight — she got back in the truck on the driver's side and pushed him toward me. Then I was able to support his shoulders and pull him free of the truck. She slid out after him and caught his feet, and together we hauled him into the house.

The fact that he slept through all of it didn't make me feel any better.

"Let's put him on the couch," I said, out of breath.

Grandma moved the recliner out of the way so we'd have a clearer path. Then she bent over him and gave him a medical once-over – looked at his eyes, took his pulse, and so on. She had worked as a nurse in Indiana until she retired. "His vitals are fine," she said, "as near as I can tell. Do you have a thermometer?"

"No," I said.

She shrugged. "It's okay. His forehead's not warm, so I doubt he has a fever anyway." She was chafing his hand as she spoke. Then she turned to me. "Does his skin feel funny to you?"

I took his hand and ran my thumb over the back of it. "That's weird. It almost feels furry."

"Furry," she echoed. "That's what I thought, too."

Suddenly, he cried out – as lost and forlorn a sound as I've ever heard anyone utter.

"Jesus, Rafe!" I bent over him. "What's wrong?"

His eyes were still closed, but now he was whispering something. I put my ear next to his lips to see if I could make out the words. When I did, it horrified me.

What he was saying was, "They got her, Dad. I'm sorry, but they got her." Over and over.

I sank to my knees and looked up at Grandma and Hilary. "There's another kushtaka. It's pretending to be Rafe's dad."

Hilary's eyes widened in fright. Grandma looked toward the door nervously and said, "I hope they get back here soon."

They were only about a half-hour behind us, but it felt like longer. At last, the door opened and our exhausted warriors trooped in. Grandma noticed Grandpa Drew clutching his side and went to him at once.

Lawson took one look at Rafe and began unpacking his medicine bag even before I could tell him what was going on. "He won't wake up," I said as he pulled his regalia out of the bag.

"What's he saying?" Auntie asked. I was still on the floor next to the couch. She came to stand beside me and put her hand on his forehead as if to stroke it. Then she hissed and drew back.

"He keeps apologizing to his father," I said. "I think there's another one of those things out there."

"No doubt," said Lawson. He was pulling things out of his bag — a drum, which he handed to Webb, and rattles, which he handed around to the rest of us. "We're going to have to to break the kushtaka's hold on him. Get his shirt off." I hurried to comply.

Hollow-eyed, Auntie went back out to the car to get her own regalia. Grandpa Drew, with Grandma supporting him, moved to stand in front of the TV. Webb scooted next to the couch where Rafe's feet were, and Hilary took the spot next to him.

Lawson looked at me kindly. "I'm going to need to be where you are," he said. Reluctantly, I got to my feet and stood next to Rafe's head, while Lawson took my former spot at about the middle of his chest. He carried a good-sized wooden jar, which he handed to me. I cradled it against my side with one hand and held a rattle at the ready with the other.

Auntie came back in and donned her regalia swiftly. Then she positioned herself between Hilary and Grandma.

Rafe was still murmuring, his eyes squinched shut. Lawson nodded to Webb, who began a heartbeat rhythm. The rest of us followed suit with the rattles, and then Lawson started in with his song — a wild thing that included motions indicating a struggle with an unseen foe.

Rafe began to toss his head and mutter more loudly. Then he, too, seemed to be fighting something off, pummeling the couch with his feet and cartwheeling his arms at the elbow.

Without breaking stride, Lawson pointed at the jar and leaned in. "Rub that stuff on his arms and legs," he said.

I set my rattle on the coffee table and pulled the stopper off the jar. The stuff within was the color and consistency of wet mud. I scooped some out and pinioned one of Rafe's arms so I could slather the ointment on it. He fought me to start with, but at the first touch of the mud, his movements became less frantic. I coated both arms to the shoulder, and then scooted around Lawson to reach Rafe's legs. I had to remove his shoes and socks first – Hilary stepped over to help me with the shoes – and then slid the mud up under his jeans to his knees, which was as far as I could easily reach.

As I stepped around Lawson again, I looked at Rafe's face, and nearly dropped the jar of ointment. His eyes were open, and he was tracking my movements with an intensity I'd never seen in him before. I set down the jar and capped it, and resumed my place next to him – and he grabbed my hand and brought it to his lips.

I think I might have said something, but I couldn't tell you what it was. I do know that I sank to the floor, put my head on his shoulder, and began to cry with relief.

Shortly thereafter, someone – Lawson, I think – helped Rafe to a sitting position. His mother came over and hugged him, and so did Grandma and Hilary. Grandpa Drew clasped his shoulder with his good hand, and dropped a kiss on the top of my head. Webb, too, gave Rafe a pat on the back while he mumbled something about how good it was to have him back. Lawson had quite a bit to say – instructions about the mud, I guess – and then realized nobody was going to remember it, so he wrote it all down on a piece of paper.

Through it all, Rafe never let go of my hand. Not even when everyone cleared out of the house in search of lunch, leaving us alone to catch up.

At one point in our conversation, Rafe said to me, "That's twice now that you've saved my life. I owe you so much, Sage."

"You don't owe me anything," I said. "You've had my back, too."

"I'll have your back forever," he said, and kissed me. Things probably would have gone much farther if the others hadn't come in at that point, bearing food. It was just burgers and fries, but nothing had ever tasted so sweet in my life.

After lunch, Grandpa Drew and Grandma hit the road for home. He was obviously sore from being mown down by the kushtaka, but he refused Grandma's suggestion to take him to a hospital. Well, okay, she did more than suggest. In fact, she said that if he didn't go, he was going to feel worse, because she was going to whack him upside the head. He dug in his heels, though, and in the end, she pulled an Ace bandage out of the first-aid kit in the truck and wrapped his torso thoroughly, all the while calling him seven kinds of a fool.

"Why spend the money?" he said when she stopped to take a breath. "You know the doc is going to do exactly what you're doing, and tell me to take something for the pain."

"Your rib could be broken, that's why," she returned.

"It's not broken," he said. "I've had a broken rib before. I know what it feels like. Ow! Not so tight, Virginia!"

"Serves you right, you old fool," she muttered, but she loosened the wrapping a little.

Not long afterward, the two of them hugged each of us in turn and headed out the door to the truck. The last thing I heard was Grandma saying, "Not with a broken rib, you're not driving," as she got in on the driver's side.

Lawson and Auntie left, too. Their flight home wasn't for another few hours, but they needed to check out of their hotel. "We've already stayed past checkout time," Auntie said as she hugged me. "We'll have to pay for another night regardless, unless they've tossed our luggage out with the trash." She grinned at me. Then she turned to Rafe and held his face between her hands. "My beautiful boy," she said softly, and engulfed him in a hug.

The old Rafe – the pre-kushtaka-attack Rafe – would have rolled his eyes in embarrassment. But this new Rafe held her as tightly as she was holding him. "Thanks for coming, Mom," he said when he released her. "I love you."

"I love you, too," she said, eyes bright with tears.

As she turned away, Lawson stepped up to shake hands. "You've got my instructions over there," he said, tilting his head toward the scrap of paper on the coffee table. "Give the mud another few hours to work before you soak it off. And for gods' sake, don't spend any more time with dead people, okay?"

Rafe ducked his head. "I won't. I promise." He raised his eyes to the older man. "Thanks for coming with Mom. I owe you."

Lawson waved him off. "You don't owe me anything, son. This is what I do."

One more round of hugs, and they were gone, too.

That left Webb, Hilary, Rafe, and me. Hilary said she ought to check on whether Enkou was back yet, and Webb volunteered to go with her.

"That's new," said Rafe, watching the two of them through the window.

"Yeah. It took him less time to get over Kerry than I thought it would."

He looked around. "That's who's missing. Where is she, anyhow?"

So I filled him in on my conversation with Aunt Shannon. "The bottom line is that I've been a total ass," I finished. "And I hope she'll forgive me eventually."

"I'm sure she will. You two have been friends for a long time."

I hoped he was right.

"Tell me about this gods' congress," he said. So I told him my big revelation, and outlined what I intended to ask the gods to help us with.

"I feel stupid now," he said. "It's so obvious. I should have figured it out before."

I shrugged. "Don't feel bad. Nobody else figured it out, either." I stared at the wall for a moment. "I just wish I knew why They didn't tell us. We could have had this thing wrapped up so much sooner if They'd just come clean."

"No idea," he said. "But I'd sure like to know the answer. Let's ask Them."

"Okay," I said, slipping my arms around his middle. "But not just yet."

"What did you have in mind for us to do in the meantime?" he asked, encircling me with his arms.

"How about this?" I asked, and kissed him.

"That will do for a start," he said, his lips moving against mine.

Things proceeded from there. At one point, I asked him whether he was up to it yet. But what I really wanted to know was whether he was over Bobbie at last.

He ignored the question I'd asked aloud. Instead, he talked about Bobbie – the real Bobbie, the one who had died in the plane crash. "We lived along the same road when we were growing up, but she didn't really ever have time for me. She was a few years older, so she had her own crowd. But she was beautiful." He shook his head at the memory, a smile playing around his lips. "She carried herself like a model – you know, that slouchy runway walk, like a panther on the prowl. She was irresistible."

I was starting to feel a little outclassed again. "But?" I prompted.

He came back to the present with a start. "Oh, well, you know. She was beautiful and she knew it. I wanted in her pants, yeah, but so did every other guy in town.

"Then came this one school dance. I was a freshman and she was a senior, so of course she already thought she was hot shit and I was nothing, right? I finally screwed up my courage and asked her to dance. And she laughed at me. We had lived on the same road for years, but it turned out she didn't know my name. I was just some random kid to her. She said she couldn't believe I was serious. And then she went off to dance with some senior boy."

"Ouch," I said.

He looked at me sideways. "Yeah, well, it hurt at the time. But eventually I realized she had done me a favor. I watched some of the other boys make fools of themselves over her, and the only ones she would have anything to do with were the boys who could do something for her."

"Sex?"

"Nah. She could have gotten that from any of us." He brushed a stray lock of hair away from my face. "What I mean is that their parents had money, or were powerful in some way. She finally ran off with a kid whose family supposedly had connections in the movie industry. The two of them went off to California not long after they both graduated from high school."

"I guess she didn't make it big," I said.

"Nope. And I guess she had finally given up and was on her way home when the plane she was on crashed."

"Sad story." I pleated the sheet between my fingers.

"Yeah, it is. But you know, she was a perfect choice for the kushtaka."

I looked up at him. "What makes you say that?"

He shrugged. "She was always a taker, right? So it fit right in with her old personality that she would be after me the way she was."

"What did she want, anyway?" I asked, turning sideways to get a better view of his face. "Why did she pick you?"

"She saw us on TV and recognized me."

"I know that," I said. "What I wonder is whether our mission swayed her. Whether she was trying to keep us from succeeding in saving the Earth."

He shook his head. "I didn't get that sense from her at all. I think it was purely an opportunistic attack."

I nodded and kissed him. But privately, I wondered about it. It seemed like a long way for a creature like a kushtaka to come, just to snag a particular victim. Particularly one whom she cared so little about when they were younger.

On the other hand, Rafe had said Bobbie was notorious for using people to get what she wanted. When she saw us on TV, she might have thought Rafe could help her become famous. For someone obsessed with fame, that would have been worth a journey of any length.

And yet, when Rafe was delirious, he had been talking to his father. I was sure of that. And by then the kushtaka known as Bobbie had been destroyed, so she shouldn't have had any further hold over Rafe. He shouldn't have been fighting off the effects of the initial attack at that point.

I thought about mentioning all this to Rafe, but he distracted me with kisses and a few other things.

Still, I couldn't help worrying that his father was still out there somewhere, biding his time, and waiting for a chance to derail our efforts again. I hoped I was wrong, but I had a bad feeling that I was right.

Walking with Hilary

Even if I hadn't been so intrigued by Hilary at that point, I would have been grateful for an excuse to get out of the house. It still reminded me too much of Kerry, even though she had been gone for days. Plus, because she was gone, I was tempted to walk into her room and rifle through her stuff, which would have been wrong for a whole bunch of reasons.

And then, too, the house had acquired a weird vibe since my arrival. Part of it was the purification ceremony that we had just wrapped up. Tlingit ceremonies are different from either Ute or Lakota ceremonies, and the purification rite was a powerful one. There was bound to be some psychic stuff hanging around the place that would bother any sensitive person. And the gods knew I was sensitive. To be honest, I didn't know how Sage could stand it.

There was also the fact that Kerry and Sage were on the outs. Apart from my feelings – or evolving feelings, maybe – about Kerry, the strain in Sage's relationship with her was also giving the house an unsettled air.

And finally, I had a sense that we weren't quite done with the kushtaka infestation. There was a predatory feeling around the place, as if someone had it in for my sister and was just lying in wait to take her out. That should have convinced me to stick around, instead of running off with Hilary. But I knew I wouldn't have been much use in a psychological battle – my talents, like Sage's, are pretty much bound to the physical plane.

Still, I should have warned her before I left. But she was getting ready to get all cozy with Rafe, and it would have been awkward to stay. And too, I wanted to know how Enkou was getting along. We hadn't heard from him since Hilary had kicked him out of the restaurant a couple of nights before. A lot had happened since then.

And yes, okay, I wanted to spend more time with Hilary. So when she said she was going to walk over to the creek to check on Enkou, I jumped at the chance to go with her.

"Look at how much snow has melted," she said at one point. She marveled at how the snowbanks that had been over her head just a few days before were now below the level of her waist.

"It helps that the Front Range is semi-arid," I said. "Snow always melts fast around here. Some of it actually evaporates."

"I know that," she said, flashing her eyes at me. "But this went away really fast." She grinned. "I'm just so proud of Enkou. This was a big job, and nobody's given him any credit for it yet."

"I'll be happy to give him plenty of credit," I said, "if we can find him."

It wasn't as hard as it could have been. He was right where Hilary expected to find him: dug into the mud at the end of a path that originally had been sliced into the snowbank on a diagonal to the creek. "Looks like somebody used a straight edge to cut this path," I said.

"Your sister did it," she said as she tried to coax Enkou out with a piece of cucumber.

"That explains it. Only an engineer would put that much precision work into a tunnel through the snow. I prefer more organic structures."

She gave me a puzzled look. "But this was the most direct route. Why is that bad?"

"Because math," I said. "Math is hard."

She laughed at me. "No, it's not! Math is logical. It makes perfect sense when you understand what's going on."

"Like I said," with a sigh.

She turned toward me from where she was crouched on the bank of the creek. "If you ever need help with math, give me a shout," she said.

"Well, thanks, but...."

"I mean it, Webb. I'd be happy to help you." Her eyes went all soft, and for a minute I wondered whether we were talking about something other than math. Then Enkou poked one arm out and snatched the cucumber chunk away from her. "Hey!" she yelled, startled. Her arms windmilled and she fell backward into the creek.

I couldn't help it; I laughed. Then I offered her a hand up. With a slightly disgusted look at both Enkou and me, she took my hand. "Ugh," she said, brushing at her backside. "Now my pants are soaked, you wretch! And it's cold out here!"

Enkou waved with the paw that had reached out for the cucumber. The rest of him was still hidden in his shell. That really set Hilary off. She spat a stream of very unflattering-sounding Japanese in the kappa's direction. I couldn't catch most of it, but I definitely heard *baka*, which means "stupid," more than once.

At last, Enkou poked his head out. In sleepy Japanese, he gave her a report on the activities of the kappa crew. From what I could make out, it sounded like they had succeeded in shifting enough snowmelt into the holding tank in Nav – and enough unmelted snow to the poles as glacier food – that life on Earth was no longer in danger. Then he said he was so tired that he intended to sleep for a week. And he pulled his head back into his shell.

"Fine," Hilary said, and stomped up the rise to the sidewalk.

I was about to follow her when Enkou put his head out again. In passable English, he said, "You good man. She like you." Then he winked at me and pulled his head back in.

Well, then. "Um. You're a good man, too. Kappa. A good kappa."

He waved again and went back to sleep.

"Are you coming?" Hilary called to me. "I need to go home and change. My butt's freezing."

"On my way," I called back, and climbed up to meet her. I wasn't sure whether having a kappa seal of approval was a good thing or a bad thing, but for now, I'd take it.

Approaching the house again, I got that same sense of foreboding I'd felt earlier – except stronger. So strong, in fact, that the hair on the back of my neck was standing at attention. "Do you feel that?" I asked Hilary.

"I can't feel anything. My butt is numb," she said with a laugh. But then she slowed. "Oh. I see what you mean." She screwed her face into a grimace of distaste.

I stopped, and touched her elbow. "Are we sure those kushtakas were after Rafe?"

"Why wouldn't they be? Who else would they be after?" Then daylight dawned. "You think they really wanted Sage?"

"I don't know," I said. "But if she's what they're after, then he's the way to get to her." I glanced at the house again. There was nothing lurking near the front door, so our friendly neighborhood kushtaka must have been on the other side of the house. "Are you up for a little game of Ring Around the Rosey?"

Her head jerked back in surprise. "Here? Now?"

"Right here and right now."

She looked at me sidelong. "You don't think we're a little old for kiddie games?"

"Not this one." I dug through the pockets of my cargo pants, finally finding what I was after in a pocket just above my left knee. I get a lot of shit from the kids at school about wearing these pants – skinny jeans are the big thing these days, so I'm just not that cool. On the other hand, bucking the fashion trend gives me plenty of places to stash yarn and other types of string for emergencies like this. "Here we go." I pulled out a ball of fishing line and began fashioning it into a sort of net. It took me about ten minutes to produce a good-sized piece of netting, maybe five feet by five feet square. I glanced up at Hilary at one point and faltered; her eyes were wide and her expression rapt as she watched me work. I had to look away from her to catch my rhythm again.

"Okay," I said at last, stuffing the rest of the line in my pocket again.

"What was that about precision engineering?" she said, one eyebrow raised.

"No, no, no," I said, trying to keep a straight face. "The part you're supposed to remember is the bit about organic shapes." I had the net bunched up in one hand, and with the other, I gestured toward Sage's house. "Let's set this up between those two trees on the side of the house. And then we'll play our game."

The net blended in nicely on top of the lingering snow. I tossed the lead over a low-hanging aspen branch, and set up the trip wire by tying it to a cable stapled to the side of the house. I stepped back for a moment to survey my work. As long as the creature didn't pull down the cable when it tripped the net, I thought it would be fine.

"Okay," I said quietly to Hilary. "Let's go around the house this way. We want it to chase us. You know where the trip wire is, right? Make sure you veer off just before you're going to hit the wire. I want the thing to have so much momentum that it can't avoid the snare."

She swallowed hard and nodded.

"How's your butt?" I asked.

She blinked at my change of subject. "It's fine."

"I don't want you getting frostbite or something."

"I'm fine," she insisted. "Let's just do this."

I nodded and we began our stroll around the house.

As I'd suspected, the critter was lying in wait behind some bushes near the back door. As soon as I saw it, I threw my hands in the air and screamed like a girl. Hilary screamed, too – largely, I suspect, because I had screamed.

Then the kushtaka slithered upright, and she screamed for real. This one was bigger than the one we'd cornered up at Bear Lake. Bigger, older-looking, and probably smarter. I hoped it hadn't been lurking in the woods when I laid my trap for the other critter. And then I realized that if it had, the wolves wouldn't have been so willing to wait her out.

All of that flashed through my mind in the split second it took me to turn around and run back the way we'd come, with Hilary just ahead of me.

Around the corner of the house the critter chased us. We were within inches of the trip when Hilary veered left, toward the trees. I followed her. The kushtaka, alas for him, could not. The cable held, and so did my net.

As the snarling creature thrashed above us, we cheered and high-fived each other. Hugging her seemed appropriate, too, so I did.

"What the hell...?" That was Sage. She and Rafe, mostly dressed and wearing coats, had apparently heard the commotion and had rounded the corner of the house from the front. "Oh, shit," she said. "There *was* another one." She reached back to Rafe, who put one arm around her shoulders and glared at the thing in the net.

"Now what do we do?" Hilary asked, slipping away from me. "Lawson's gone home."

Rafe's mouth was set in a grim line. "I'll be right back." He disappeared around the corner again, and I heard the front door shut.

The thing was still growling and trying to cut the fishing line with its paws when Rafe returned, clutching a Swiss army knife. The kushtaka saw the short blade and began making a low, throaty sound that I suspected was meant to be a laugh.

Rafe ignored the monster in the net. He held the blade before him and began a Tlingit song in a sure, calm voice.

The kushtaka recoiled. Then, in an educated male voice, it said, "Rafe, son. Don't do this to me. Don't do this to your own father."

Rafe kept going until he ended the song. Then he looked the creature in the eye and said, "Nice try," as he took aim and let the knife fly.

His throw was true. The short blade embedded itself in the monster's left eye and worked its way deeper. With an unearthly howl of anguish, the kushtaka convulsed twice and went limp.

"It's dead?" Sage asked. "It's really dead?"

"It's really dead," Rafe said. Then, his reserves depleted, his knees buckled. Sage caught one arm and I stepped across to catch the other, and together we managed to get him back into the house.

"I'm fine," he mumbled as we hauled him to the couch. "Just need to rest."

"And eat," Sage said. "I bet you haven't eaten since dinner Saturday night." She looked pointedly at Hilary, who hurried off to the kitchen.

"Don't remember."

"There's a can of chicken soup," Hilary called. "Is that okay, Rafe?"

But he was already asleep. Sage and I traded a look that said, *what next?* But neither of us was dumb enough to say it aloud.

Rafe slept for an hour or so, and then woke up enough for Sage to spoon some of the chicken soup into him. That revived him sufficiently to talk about what had happened. "There were two of them," he said. "I remember now. The second one drove the car that took us up to Estes Park. I was pretty much out of it by then, but I remember the driver leaving for some reason." His voice trailed off. Then he looked at Sage with alarm. "Wait. He was coming back here for you."

"I knew it," I said. "They probably wanted Sage all along. You were just the conduit to her."

He nodded in confirmation of what I'd said, but his next words were addressed to my sister. "They wanted to kill me and turn me, so they could get to you."

She stared at him for a moment, letting it sink in. Then, "Fuck," she said. "Who do you think is behind this?"

Rafe shrugged helplessly. "I don't know. It could have been my father, but…." He shrugged again.

"Well, if it was," I said, "he's not going to be a threat any longer." I clapped him on the shoulder, and he nodded and looked away.

"How horrible," said Hilary. "To hate someone so much that you would come back from the dead to get even with them."

Rafe and Sage looked at one another. Then she got up from the couch and began to pace. "I only met the man once!" she said, flinging her hands up for emphasis. "Why would he hate me?"

"It's not you, honey," Rafe said. "It's what you stand for. You ruined his life's work."

"Yeah, well, his life's work was shit," she spat. "You know that as well as I do."

"Doesn't mean it wasn't important to him." Rafe's tone of voice was mild, and held no rebuke. In hearing it, her anger collapsed. I marveled at the way he managed her moods. No one in our family had ever been able to get the hang of it, except maybe Grandfather.

"Anyway," I said, "it's over."

"Yeah," said Sage, her shoulders slumping as she resumed her seat on the couch.

"Want more soup?" Hilary asked Rafe. He took the bowl from her and helped himself.

Not long afterward, I went outside to see what sort of mess was left for us to clean up.

There was none. All that remained was a powdery residue on the snow below the empty and undamaged net, and Rafe's Swiss army knife embedded, point down, in the ground.

Chapter 13

I wasn't sure Rafe would be up to attending the meeting with the gods, given the weekend he'd had. But he rallied. He said he wouldn't dream of letting me go up against Them without being there.

"I meant what I said," he told me. "I'm with you to the end on this. Nothing will keep me from your side."

I'm not going to lie – his words warmed my heart. But at the same time, I wondered how realistic the sentiment was. I could envision any number of scenarios in which we could be separated, either by our own choice or by some force beyond our control.

But when I mentioned that to him, he dug in his heels and said, "Nope. Ain't gonna happen. You're not going to get rid of me that easily."

I stopped arguing with him, but it didn't mean I was convinced.

Shortly before five o'clock, Cerridwen appeared before us. Rafe and I were still on the living room couch, where we'd been ever since he'd collapsed. Webb had turned on the TV and plugged in one of his video games, and Hilary was watching him play. Personally, I could've used some peace and quiet, but I was comfortable next to Rafe, and he didn't seem inclined to move, either.

And then Cerridwen showed up and spoiled it. "All is in readiness," She said, looking pleased with Herself.

"Now?" After the numerous brushes with death and disaster we'd had over the past few weeks, I was ready for a break. "Can we put it off 'til tomorrow?"

Her brow lowered until She was glaring at me through narrow slits. "You called this meeting. Now you would dare to keep the gods waiting?" She thundered.

Webb had paused his game. Now he looked at me with mirth in his eyes. "Well, when She puts it *that* way…"

I sighed, and patted Rafe's knee. "You okay?"

"Yeah," he sighed. "Let's get this over with."

Damn. Nobody was going to let me off the hook. On the other hand, I'd never reacted well when someone tried to bully me, and I wasn't in any mood to change that now. "Do you know what we've been through over the past forty-eight hours?" I asked. I swear I didn't yell at Her, although I might have raised my voice a little. "We've killed two kushtakas who were trying to turn Rafe into one of them. And last week, we saved the world from a flood of epic proportions. Rafe also almost died then. Don't we deserve an afternoon off?"

Cerridwen's expression hadn't changed. If She'd been a thunder goddess, I was pretty sure the heavens would have already opened on our heads. "Do you know what your mother was going through when she mediated the agreement that led to the Second Coming?" She asked, Her tone deceptively mild.

I traded a mystified look with Webb. "No. I mean, I guess not. What was she going through?"

"She was in labor with you."

I blinked. Mom had never cared to share this bit of family lore with us. "In labor? The whole time?" At the goddess's nod, I said, "But it went on for days, didn't it?"

Cerridwen ignored my question. "And right before that," She went on, "she nearly died at the hands of her kidnappers."

"Mom was *kidnapped?*" Webb said, his eyes wide. "Did you know that, Sage?"

"No," I said, and looked at Rafe. He'd nearly died twice in my place. And if Mom had nearly died while she was pregnant with me, that meant *I* had nearly died, too, before I was even born.

I was beginning to realize just what a privileged princess I was. If I'd seen someone else behaving the way I had, I'd have been tempted to go all roasty-toasty on them.

My cheeks burning, I said, "Sorry." It wasn't enough, but it was a start. "Let's go, you guys."

"That's better," said Cerridwen, mollified. One blink and we were there.

We stood on the vast plain I recognized from previous forays into the gods' universe. The Slavs called the gods' land Prav; the Norse, Valhalla. The Lakota believed it was beyond the Milky Way. In my parents' cosmogony, it translated into the sort of barren desert plain you might find in the southwestern United States. Distant mountains ringed the perimeter, and billions upon billions of stars shone brightly overhead, lighting the plain as brightly as the sun.

Benches or pews had been brought in from somewhere, and gods sat upon them – rows upon uncounted rows of deities from every pantheon ever. The benches were arranged in a circle around a central ceremonial fire. I recognized the layout – my mother used it when she conducted her mediations. But there were no chairs inside the circle, as there would have been for a mediation. Instead, the four of us – Rafe, Webb, Hilary, and I – stood alone next to the fire.

Cerridwen hugged me. "You'll do fine," She said, and took a seat in the front row next to Brighid, who waved at us. She had been the one to heal Rafe when his father had tried to turn him into a giant iceworm. I noted a few more familiar faces in Their row: White Buffalo Calf Pipe Woman, Loki, Thor, and Diana; Morrigan, Nanabush, Gaia, and Jesus; Jehovah; and Perun, Veles, and Benzaiten. So I wasn't surprised to notice box seats next to Them for the other humans in attendance: my mother and father; Grandfather, looking even more frail than the last time I'd seen him; Darrell Warren and Tess Showalter, and their friends Sue and Robbie Duckworth; Rafe's brother Paul; and Antonia Greco, the First Lady of the United States, with her husband, President Brock Holt.

"Holy shit," I heard Webb mutter under his breath. "The gang's all here." Then he punched me in the shoulder. "Knock 'em dead, sis."

"Shut up," I told him under my breath. I looked around for a microphone, but there wasn't one.

"Just talk," Mom said, her tone encouraging. "They'll all hear you."

Well, she would know. It's not like she hadn't done this before.

I took a moment to organize my thoughts. I hadn't rehearsed what I intended to say – it wasn't as if I'd had time – so my first line was a bit more of a show-stopper than I'd intended for it to be: "It has come to our attention that You guys have been holding out on us."

You could have heard a pin drop on that plain. I scanned the faces of the deities before me. Some seemed surprised. Some appeared to be affronted. Only Cerridwen looked smug.

If I'd looked at the box where my parents and the others sat, I would have lost my nerve. So I didn't. Instead, I pressed on. "One of Your messages to humanity, right after the Second Coming, was that there was nothing You could do to stop climate change. It was all on us, You said. Earth is a closed system, You said. And so we made all the internal changes You told us to make. Over the past twenty years, with Your help and encouragement, we have transitioned away from fossil fuels wherever possible. We gave up on nuclear power because You told us the potential cost to the environment was too great. Even without it, we are now at the point where approximately ninety-eight percent of the power consumption on Earth comes from renewable sources – solar, wind, and water.

"But as You know, it's not enough. We didn't change our ways fast enough, or maybe You returned to Earth too late. It doesn't really matter at this point. Because either way, the damage humanity did to Earth's climate is still playing out – and will continue to play out for perhaps another eighty to a hundred years. Our seas are rising, and coastlines around the world are shifting inland. Our deserts are drier. Our glaciers are disappearing. Our storms are more severe. And all of this will keep happening until we figure out a way to mitigate the damage that has already occurred." Out of the corner of my eye, I caught Gaia looking worried as She caressed Her Earth-shaped belly.

"We're working on that," I went on, "but as You know, it's been slow going. We've found that it's not that easy to pull carbon dioxide and other greenhouse gases out of the atmosphere and sequester them. Carbon sinking is time-consuming, and expensive to develop. It takes a lot of research. It requires a convenient, easy-to-reach place to store the carbon and other pollutants. And we're running out of time.

"You told us You couldn't help. You said Earth is a closed system. You lied."

The collective godly gasp made quite a breeze. "We did not lie!" proclaimed Jehovah.

"We might have stretched the truth a little, here and there," Nanabush said with a shrug. "But lie? That's a pretty hefty charge."

"I can back it up," I said, taking Rafe's hand. "My team and I have spent the last several weeks trying to do this alone. I will grant you that we've made some missteps." I noticed for the first time that Enkou was with us – literally. He stood next to Hilary, instead of taking his place among the gods. "And we've done what we could to mitigate our mistakes. But in the process, we discovered that the Earth is not a closed system."

"How so?" President Holt asked.

I turned to him. "Mr. President, maybe it looks like a closed system from the gods' perspective, but there are parts of the system that aren't readily apparent to human perception." I nodded to Tess. "One of the mistakes we made was in not taking into account the effects of the World Tree. As you know, many cultures believe in some structure – either natural or human-made – that serves as a backbone for all creation, linking the world of the gods with the Underworld and with our reality on Earth. We learned this structure actually exists. And it's more than just a conduit for the gods to get from Their world to ours, or for humanity's dead to get from our world to the afterlife. The World Tree also helps to regulate Earth's climate by participating in the hydrologic cycle."

"Well, of course," Veles said, looking down His nose at us. "Everyone knows that."

"Maybe all the gods know it," I told him, "but humans don't." I turned back to President Holt. "We only discovered it when Veles told us to stop trying to keep the World Tree's taproot out of the catchment pond in Nav. We needed the tree's help to put the water back into the hydrologic cycle gradually. We humans couldn't do it on our own. When we tried, we botched it. But nobody told us the system had a failsafe." I looked out over the vast sea of deific faces before us. "Nobody ever told humanity it was even an option."

I could see some of the gods squirming in Their seats.

Finally, "We never thought about it," Jesus admitted. "You're right, Sage. When We talk about Earth being a closed system, it's natural for Us to include Our realms and the afterlife in that system. It's easy for Us to forget that We have a different perspective on the Earth than humanity does. Even *I* forget."

Jehovah leaned forward and gave His son a sympathetic look. "Do not be too hard on Yourself. It has been a long time since You were human."

While this exchange was going on, I glanced at President Holt. He seemed to be ignoring the gods' self-flagellation in favor of pursuing another line of thought. My perception was confirmed when he asked, "So what does this mean in terms of climate change? Does your team have a solution?"

"Maybe not," I said. "But we have a process we'd like to try. What we need is a really big area where we can experiment with removing the CO_2 from the atmosphere, and an even bigger area — one similar in size to the catchment pond in Nav — where we can store the material that we hope will result from our process."

Darrell leaned back in his chair and looked toward the gods. "What do You think, Nanabush? Have You got a candidate for that?"

"I do," said Pele, rising from Her seat. Her molten hair streamed down Her back. "But it will take quite a bit of work to reopen the tunnels."

Dad's eyes flew open. "You mean the ones under Grandfather's old place? The ones that collapsed when we fled from Coatlicue?"

Pele? Coatlicue? Webb and I exchanged a startled glance. Clearly a whole lot had happened to our parents that we knew nothing about. "How about you fill us in on what you're talking about?" I said.

Dad ducked his head. "Sorry. We spared you both a lot of the details."

"Like the part about how Mom almost died when she was carrying me?"

He looked stunned. "Who told you that?"

"Cerridwen." I gestured toward Her.

He looked back and forth between us, and daylight dawned on his face. "Ah. Well, congratulations to both of you."

"The details, Dad," Webb prompted.

"Right." And Dad launched into this shaggy-dog story about how Loki had frog-marched him, Mom, Aunt Shannon, Uncle George, and a couple of other guys into the entrance to the Mexica underworld, which was conveniently located in a cave a short distance from Grandfather's wickiup. Loki had hoped to use the portal to reach the Norse underworld and free Odin's son Baldur, who had died due to one of Loki's practical jokes. Odin had been so incensed over Baldur's death that He had banished Loki to an eternity of suffering, and Loki had hoped that if Baldur came back to life, Odin would release Him from His sentence. It didn't work, but Odin freed Loki anyway. However, the ploy rattled Coatlicue, an Aztec goddess who had been chained to a root of the World Tree that reached into the cavern. Coatlicue wanted to get Her hands on Mom – Dad was vague about why, exactly – and to allow them to escape, one of the guys with them called on Pele to fill the cavern with molten lava. Which She did.

"Wow," Rafe said. I agreed. It made our run-in with the kushtakas sound like a piñata party.

"You guys need to write this all down someday," Webb said. "I bet there's more you haven't told us."

Mom and Dad exchanged a look. "Maybe I will," Mom said.

"Anyway," I said, making a stab at getting the meeting back on track, "You're saying You might be able to reopen those tunnels and caverns for us?"

"Perhaps," Pele said. "But it is not something We could do overnight. Clearing the lava out alone will take Us at least a day or two. And then there is the question of what to do with Coatlicue's remains."

"She escaped," said a new voice – that of a feathered serpent who rose from His seat a few rows back. "My brother and I have installed Her in a different part of the caverns. She will not trouble You or Your efforts, Pele."

"Thank You, Quetzalcoatl," Pele said. "That is good to hear." As He nodded and resumed His seat, She turned back to us. "Can you give Us three days? That should be sufficient time to clear out enough space for your purposes."

I looked at my team and shrugged. "Sure. We need to make some preparations ourselves, anyway."

"Good," said Cerridwen as She rose from Her seat. She faced Her fellow gods and goddesses and said, "Thank You for coming, everyone. Let's all pitch in to get this done. We have left the stewardship of Earth's ecosystem to humanity for far too long. It's time We did our part to save the Earth."

I heard a little grumbling at Her words – it was pretty obvious that not all of the gods thought They'd been shirking Their duty to the planet – but most seemed chastened, if gods can ever be said to be chastened. In any case, They rose, congregated in smaller groups, and faded away while discussing Their plans to help.

Soon enough, the only people left on the plain were people. Humans, I mean. Well, and Enkou. And Cerridwen, who had apparently drawn the short straw and was in charge of getting us all back home.

Antonia gave Tess a big hug, which reminded me that they had worked together at NWNN before President Holt won the White House. "You look great," Tess said. "How are the boys? I mean, I see them on TV sometimes, but…"

"They're growing like weeds," Antonia said with a laugh. "And twice as much trouble. But that's off the record, of course." They both laughed. "How's your little girl?"

"Oh, Tory's doing great. She just turned seven, and she's got Daddy wrapped around her little finger."

"They do, at that age," Antonia said. Then she noticed me watching them, and beckoned to me. "Sage! I'm sure Tess would like to talk to you."

"She already has, once," I told her.

"I know – Brock and I saw the interview," the First Lady said, which freaked me out a little. "But if I know Tess, she'll want to talk to you again very soon."

"Talk to her?" Tess said, taking up the baton. "Hell, I want an exclusive!"

"Of course you do," said Mom as she approached us, hugging each of them in turn. Then she turned to me, her eyes shining. "I just wanted to…" she began, her voice cracking with emotion. "I'm just so proud of you, honey." And she gave me a hug.

I didn't know what to say. All I could do was hug her back. Mom's approval meant more to me even than knowing the President and the First Lady had seen me on TV.

Then Sue Duckworth wandered over, and another round of hugs ensued. As she let me go, she said, "I just want you to know how much Gaia and I appreciate what you're doing." Sue was pledged to Gaia, even though her husband was an Episcopal priest. "And I'm very impressed that you figured out that miscommunication. It never occurs to *any* of Them that humans see this world in a different way than They do."

"They have Their own ways of helping," I said, feeling conciliatory now that the meeting was over. "And Gaia was a big help to me when I was lost in Alaska. If it hadn't been for Her, we might have lost Rafe."

She smiled. "I heard a little bit about that. I'm glad you both survived."

President Holt took his wife by the elbow. "I've got to get back, honey," he said. "Got a country to run, and all that." Ever the politician, he shook hands with each of us. "Nice to see you all again. Naomi, any time you and Joseph want a White House tour, let us know."

"Thanks, Brock," Mom said. I had the distinct feeling that she didn't ever intend to take him up on the offer.

"Sage, good luck with your project," he said. "Keep me posted, won't you?"

"Of course," I said in surprise, and wondered how the hell I was supposed to do that.

"We'll be in touch," said Antonia, and together they faded from sight.

Mom shook her head. "Is it wrong that I still want to be Antonia when I grow up?"

"You want to be married to Brock?" Dad teased her as the men joined us. He slipped an arm around her shoulders and said, "I thought we talked about that."

"Be quiet, you," Mom said, and kissed him. They shared a look for a moment. Then she turned to Rafe and me. "I guess you two have your marching orders. Webster, are you coming with us, or going back to Boulder?"

"Home," he said. "I need to get a change of clothes."

Chapter 14

We were all surprised by how late it was when we got back. And as our day had started well before dawn, Rafe and I said goodnight to Hilary and headed off to my room together. Which sounds racy, I know, but we were both too tired to do anything but fall asleep in each other's arms. My last coherent thought was that the gods had bought us some time. Maybe, I thought, we'd be able to spend part of the next three days resting up for the next phase, instead of lurching from one disaster to the next.

It didn't happen, of course.

We were awakened by our phones chirping at the same time. "What now?" I muttered as I rolled over to check mine.

"I bet it's Martin," Rafe said.

At that moment, Hilary knocked on my door. "Hey, good morning," she called from the other side of the door. "Did y'all see the email from Dr. Raymond?"

I groaned. "You win," I told him as I started to get out of bed.

"Not so fast," he said, catching me around the hips with one arm and pulling me back. Then he called, "We saw it. We'll be out in a few minutes."

"Okay," Hilary said. I could almost hear her rolling her eyes. "I'll be in the shower."

"But it sounded urgent," I murmured, relaxing back into him as he planted tiny kisses along the side of my neck.

"So's this," he said. And that was pretty much the last coherent thing either one of us said for a little while.

Luckily for us, Dr. Raymond's message was just garden-variety urgent, not the-world-is-ending urgent. We had plenty of time to get breakfast and head over to the lab.

Once we got there, we began to realize the enormity of the task before us. We had a pretty good idea about how much CO_2 we would have to pull from the atmosphere to make a dent. What we didn't know was how much we would be able to sequester at a time, because we had no idea how big these caverns would be.

Even my parents, who had been there, were no help. "Big," Mom said, when I connected with them on Skype. "I don't know how big, but we walked forever to get there."

"And we only saw part of the cavern complex," said Dad. "There had to be at least one back entrance to the chamber we were in, because Quetzalcoatl and Tezcatlipoca used it to get Coatlicue out." He shrugged. "Sorry, honey."

"That's okay," I said, even though it wasn't, really. "We'll just run lots of scenarios."

Which we had to do anyway, because we also didn't know how efficient my power would prove to be. "I've got an estimate," Hilary said that first day, "but it's based on your output over Greenland."

"Throw it out," I said, horrified. "I don't intend to ever go that crazy again."

So that was another variable we had to throw into the mix. Building and running all of the scenarios took us the better part of those three days.

But that wasn't the worst part. The worst part was that in every damned one of them, the whole thing eventually fell apart. Either I didn't have enough juice, or there was something inherently wrong with the process Rafe was proposing that we use.

On day two, as yet another run fell apart before our eyes, Rafe pointed to the collapse and said, "That's where the miracle occurs." He was making a joke to try to lighten the mood, but I could tell he didn't think it was funny. None of us did.

We were all pretty disheartened by the time Webb arrived the next evening – the night before our spectacular failure was scheduled to happen. "Wow," he said as he plopped his backpack on the floor next to the broken dinette chair. "You guys are a barrel of laughs."

"You could just go back home," I said, from my spot next to Rafe on the couch. "You don't have to stay here and watch us make fools of ourselves tomorrow. Why *are* you here, anyway?"

"I asked him to come," Hilary said. Until Webb walked in, she had been sitting on the recliner with her knees drawn up to her chin, staring silently at nothing. Now she unbent and walked over to him, linking her arm through his. "I thought he deserved to be here. To see it through with us."

"It won't help," I said. "We're still going to go down in flames."

"Don't be so sure," he said, with that infuriatingly mysterious air of his.

"Oh, don't start that shit," I said. I hauled myself upright and went to the kitchen in search of something to drink. I was aiming for tea, but if I stumbled on something alcoholic on the way, I wouldn't have minded.

Rafe was on the same wavelength as I was. "Is there any beer?" he called.

"No, unfortunately," I said. "And there are hardly any cucumbers, either." I closed the fridge door. "Did Enkou fly the coop, Hilary?"

"He's coming back," she said. "He said he had something to do that would take a few days, so I didn't bother stocking up again. They go bad so fast at this time of year."

I stared at her for a moment. "Enkou," I said.

"What about him?" asked Hilary.

Rafe had the beginnings of a grin. "He's our wild card."

"We never accounted for him in any of our scenarios," I said. "If he can supply us with enough water…"

"And why couldn't he? He's a kappa!" Hilary's smile lit her whole face. She tugged on my brother's arm. "Come on, Webb. Help me run this scenario again."

"Oh, now, if it involves math, you're asking the wrong guy," he said, staying put.

"I'll do all the math," she said, still tugging. "I just want you to backstop me."

"Fine," he said, and allowed himself to be pulled down the hall. "'Tis a far, far better thing I do…" He winked at me just before disappearing down the hall.

Rafe levered himself off the couch, and I joined him in watching the two of them go into Hilary's room and shut the door. "You think they'll be doing any math?" he asked me, waggling his eyebrows.

"Gods," I said, slapping him gently on the shoulder. "You men are all alike."

"Ten bucks says we don't see 'em again for at least a couple of hours."

"You know that's my little brother you're talking about, right?"

"Ten bucks. You in?"

"You bet I'm in," I said. "He's only seventeen, Rafe."

"Your point?"

I rolled my eyes and went to make tea. We sat at the dinette and drank it, chatting about nothing, and waiting.

About forty-five minutes later, two voices erupted in cheering from the direction of Hilary's room. Then it got really, really quiet.

At the two-hour mark, Rafe made a show of checking his phone. With a wicked grin, he said, "Pay up."

"Gods," I said, as I pulled out my own phone and transferred the cash to him. "My parents had better never find out about this."

"My lips are sealed," he said.

Webb seemed unusually chipper the next morning at breakfast, although whether it was from whatever exercise he and Hilary might have gotten the night before, or from something else, he wasn't sharing.

He did, however, have a suggestion. "You know," he said as he poured milk on a sugary cereal-like substance that I didn't even know we had, "there's one thing you guys haven't done that would make your calculations easier."

"Yeah?" Rafe said. "What?"

Bowl in hand, Webb swung one long leg over the back of his dinette chair and sat. "You could run up to Grandfather's old place and see how the gods are getting on." He spooned cereal into his mouth while Rafe, Hilary, and I sat up straighter and traded *why didn't we think of that?* looks.

"What if They kick us out?" I said.

Webb took another bite of cereal and washed it down with orange juice. "Then you'd be no worse off than you are now."

"I think It's worth a try," Rafe said.

"Where did you find that stuff, anyway?" I asked my brother.

"Why? Did you want some?" He held out a spoonful invitingly.

I made a face. "Thanks, but no."

"It's not mine," Hilary said, pouring herself some coffee. "It must be Kerry's."

Webb paused, his mouth wide open to receive the next spoonful, which hovered in front of his mouth. Then he ate it, after all. "Serves her right," he said, after swallowing. "She ought to be here to defend her territory. How soon do you want to leave?"

I drained my coffee mug and stood. "Any time you're ready. I can't stand to sit here for another second and watch you eat that crap."

The mention of Kerry's name reminded me that I still hadn't heard from her. This was getting ridiculous. I made a mental note that once all of this was over, I would drive to her house and park myself on her doorstep until she came out to talk.

Assuming the world still existed once all of this was over. I was fully aware of the fact that we had the capacity to fail spectacularly, and take Earth down with us. I hoped the gods wouldn't let us get that far, but Their track record on that score so far left something to be desired.

Webb insisted on driving. Hilary rode shotgun, which meant Rafe and I had the back seat to ourselves. I kept looking back and forth between my brother and my roommate. She had the Japanese schoolgirl look pegged – all she needed was the pleated skirt and knee socks. He was tall and broad-shouldered, although that was due more to genetics than any athletic effort on his part. Anyway, he towered over her. They should look more mismatched, I thought. And yet they didn't.

"What?" Rafe asked me, and I realized I'd been shaking my head.

"Nothing," I told him. To be fair, he and I didn't look like a matched set, either. We were both tall, but there the similarity ended. He was handsome and well-built, and I was…smart.

I stared out the window. Then I said to Webb, "You know where you're going, right? You remember how to get there?"

"Yeah, it's…" He paused. "Maybe not."

"That's what I figured. You were pretty young the last time we were up there." I scanned the road ahead. "Take the next right. I'm pretty sure that's it."

It was. The wooden sign with the bear on it was faded and hung at a crazy angle, but it still marked the entrance to the old place. "Hang on," Webb said as he made the turn and headed up the hill. Dad had offered more than once to get someone out here to make the driveway smoother, and maybe even reroute it so that it didn't feel like you were driving straight up the side of a mountain. But Grandfather said he liked it the way it was. He said it weeded out the people who weren't serious about having an authentic sweat lodge experience.

The old parking area was overgrown with weeds. The whole site, in fact, had gone to seed. There was no indication of where Grandfather's wickiup had been, or the fire pit for the sweat lodge, or anything. It was just a clearing with a sheer drop on one side, and a killer view of the plains.

"The path is back this way," Webb said, heading toward the farthest point from the drop. I gave the plains another glance over my shoulder as we straggled after him. "At least, I think it's this way. Maybe we should have brought a machete."

"Here," I said, heading toward what looked like a game trail. "I think this is the trailhead." I struck out and hoped the others would follow me. "Are we going all the way up to the meadow?" I called back to Webb.

"Dad said there's another entrance that's closer. But the turnoff is hard to find."

"Terrific," I muttered. Then a rumbling, thudding noise caught my attention. I turned left, toward the sound, and the path appeared before me as if by magic. "I think I found it," I said, and waited for the others to catch up.

Now everyone heard the sounds that had made me stop. "If that's not a godly construction project," Rafe said, "then I'm not sure I want to know what it is."

I gave him a crooked smile and stepped onto the side trail.

The noise got louder until it was almost deafening. Then, "Ho!" someone called, and it all stopped just as we rounded a corner to behold the mouth of the cave. Standing at the entrance was a red-haired god with a kind face that shone like the sun. "Come to see Our handiwork, have you?" He asked. Then He cupped one hand to His mouth and called into the cave, "Heracles! We've company!"

A blond giant who was built like a weightlifter came out to peer at us. "So We have, Lugh. So We have." He stuck out a meaty paw. "Pleased to have you with Us. Have you come to see the progress?"

"That's precisely why we're here," said Rafe. "And also to get an idea of how much space we'll have to work with."

"Oh, you'll have plenty of space, you will," said the Celtic god of light with a laugh. "Come on in. We've made some modifications from Naomi's time."

I ducked inside the cave and my jaw dropped. *Modifications* hardly did the project justice. Mom had said they'd walked for a long time before they got down to the cavern complex, but there was neither path nor tunnel any longer – only a vast, empty space.

"How big?" Rafe asked Lugh.

"How many cubic kilometers, would You say, Heracles?"

The big guy shrugged. "Four hundred, maybe?"

Rafe whistled. "That's almost a hundred cubic miles."

"Is it big enough, do you think?" Lugh asked, concerned.

I had to laugh. "Oh, yeah," I said. "This should work just fine."

"Good," He said with a decisive nod. "And you'll have five times this much space for your storage needs. We're putting in a chute at the bottom of the cavern that leads directly there."

"Inconceivable," Rafe said, looking up. I followed his gaze with my own eyes, and realized I couldn't see the ceiling – it vanished into the shadows high above us.

"Just let Us get finished with the last bits here," Lugh told us. "I'll send Cerridwen along when all is in readiness." And He showed us back to the mouth of the cave.

"Well," I said when we were back outside in daylight, "I guess we're really going to have to do this. The gods have gone to an awful lot of trouble for us." I turned to Rafe, who looked bemused. "You okay?"

"I just never..." He shook his head. "It was all just a little idea I had. I never imagined anything like this."

I glanced back at the cave. "To be honest, neither did I." And now I wondered if we could pull it off, after all. I had no doubt the process would work. But was I up to the challenge?

I looked at Rafe again, and my trepidation grew. It was one thing to disappoint the world, but quite another to ruin my boyfriend's big dream. I wasn't sure which one I dreaded more.

What really happened behind that closed door

I know what you're thinking. It's the same thing Rafe and Sage thought. But you're wrong. Hilary and I didn't have sex, okay?

I mean, we might have. She was pretty excited about finding the hole in the team's calculations, and ecstatic when the scenario worked, at last. And she was awfully cute when she was ecstatic. I couldn't help but give her a hug. It lasted a long time, and there might have been kissing involved. But we never got any farther because then Enkou showed up.

That kappa has the worst timing.

Anyway, what followed was a long explanation – in rapid-fire Japanese, broken English, and pantomime – of what Enkou and his kappa army intended to do. There was still a fair amount of water in the catchment basin in Nav – the World Tree was still in the process of returning it to the Earth's hydrologic cycle. So Enkou and his buddies had rigged up a way to get some of that water into the cavern the gods had cleared out – enough so that Sage could do her thing.

So the good news was that Enkou was on our side, and he stood ready and able to assist my sister and her team with their plans to save the Earth. The neither-good-nor-bad news is that I didn't get into bed with Hilary – although I admit that I was pretty frustrated when Enkou first showed up. Like I said before, if we hadn't been interrupted, who knows what would have happened?

But the really bad news is that Sage was out ten bucks, even though she'd won the bet. And the bad news for her was that I wasn't going to tell her. After all, I had my studly image to think about.

Chapter 15

I woke up well before the alarm, with all of my inadequacies banging around inside my head. Today was the day — the day I was going to save the Earth — but I was suddenly sure that I was not ready. Not prepared. Not the right person, or the right person/deity hybrid, or whatever the hell I was. And I sure didn't have enough of a handle on my puny powers to effect any sort of change on a global scale. I mean, I could maybe have a local effect, but that was it.

And then I thought about what had happened in Greenland, and realized that even if I *did* have an effect, it was likely to go horribly wrong.

Everything we had touched so far had gone horribly wrong. And when we tried to fix our mistakes, the fix went horribly wrong, too. We just didn't know enough. *I* didn't know enough. And I didn't have enough experience. All those years I'd spent being a brat and denying my powers were going to come back to bite me in the ass. And it was going to happen today.

I was going to fail, and fail spectacularly. In front of the gods and everybody.

I turned onto my side and gazed at Rafe. He was still asleep — my feverish feelings of failure hadn't been restless enough to awaken him — and it was clear that no sense of inadequacy marred *his* rest. He had pulled the ever-present elastic out of his hair before he went to sleep, and his hair now fanned out on the pillow and bunched up under his cheek. He looked relaxed. Carefree.

I realized I was crying when I felt the first drops trail across the bridge of my nose.

My sniffling must have woken him up. "Hey," he said sleepily, wiping my tears away with his thumb. "What's wrong?"

"Everything," I said, and dumped all my worries onto him. "But the worst of it is that I'm going to fail *you*," I said, blubbering now. I reached behind me for a tissue from the box on the nightstand, and sat up to blow my nose.

His hand made slow circles on my back. "Failing me is worse than failing the Earth?" he asked. "I'm honored, I think."

"You know what I mean." I tossed the tissue on the nightstand and lay back down. "It's worse because I love you. I don't want to be the thing that ruins everything for you."

He was chuckling softly. "You aren't going to ruin anything for me."

"But if this fails…"

"Then we try something else. Right?"

I blinked.

He slipped an arm under my shoulders and pulled me close. "Look. I know there's a lot of pressure on you to live up to that stupid prophecy. And it doesn't help that Webb is here in your face, reminding you of the damned thing with his smarmy know-it-all expression every time you turn around."

"Yeah. Problem is, though, he really *does* know it all."

"Doesn't matter. What matters is that you're buying into it."

I pulled back, incredulous. "What do you mean, I'm buying into it?"

"What I'm trying to say is that everything you do – every action you take – doesn't have to be loaded with portent." He pulled me back against him again. I resisted for a second before giving in, realizing I wanted to be close to him more than I wanted to fight his challenge to my worldview. "Maybe today will be the day you save the Earth. Maybe it won't. Maybe my project will work, and maybe it will need refining. That's why it's called an experiment. Right?"

What he said did make some sense. "But –"

He put a finger to my lips. "But if you ask me, you've already succeeded."

I kissed his finger before pulling his hand away and lacing my fingers through his. "How do you figure that?"

"You got the gods to admit that They were holding out on us. Granted, it wasn't intentional. But They admitted that They haven't been telling us everything. You got Them to see the hole in Their thinking, and now They're onboard with us. That's huge, Sage." He tightened his embrace. "I don't think you realize how huge it is because you're focused on the magic. But maybe the laser eyes and the flying are just window dressing. Maybe you've already saved the Earth."

I felt dizzy – as if something in my head had been wrenched out of its old slot and was trying to settle into a new one. *Done? Already saved...?* "Keep talking," I said, and burrowed my face into his neck.

He laughed softly. "You like where I'm going with this, huh?"

"I'm entertaining the possibility. Go on."

I felt him shrug. "Well. If I'm right, and I'm pretty sure I am...."

"Hubris," I said, and poked him in the belly.

He grabbed my hand and held it fast. "If I'm right," he said, "then this experiment today is more than just a demonstration project for rolling back climate change." He slid his arm out from under me and propped himself up on one elbow, his face alight. "The gods have been running the show up to now, right? Ever since the Second Coming, They've focused on teaching us the right way to live in harmony with the planet and with each other."

"Sometimes They've been a little more persuasive than others," I said, putting one hand behind my head. I was a lot more comfortable with this topic than I had been earlier.

"Sometimes They've been more than persuasive," he said, cocking his head. I had to agree. "But the point is They've been running a dictatorship. A benevolent dictatorship, for the most part – we're free to disagree with Them – but still, a dictatorship. They've been calling all the shots."

"Right. So?"

"So this time," he said, "They're taking direction from *us*. From you and me and Hilary. That hasn't happened since..."

"Since my mother mediated the Second Coming agreement," I said.

"This may be the start of a new era of working together. A new era of cooperation between the gods and humanity."

I considered this. "Do you think this was what They had in mind all along?"

"No idea," he said. "Do the gods think that far ahead?"

I snorted. "Supposedly, They made us in Their image. What do *you* think?"

He grinned. "I think They play it by ear as often as we do. So about today." He kissed the back of my hand. "Don't sweat it if the process doesn't work on the first try. Or the second. It's important that we succeed eventually, of course. But our goal today is to train the gods to work with us."

"We're not just saving the Earth," I said. "We're gaining the trust of the gods."

"Exactly," he said, and kissed my hand again. "You think you can do that?"

"It's a little less daunting than saving the planet, as goals go," I admitted. "Yeah, I think I can do that."

"I think so, too," he said, and kissed me. Then he leaned past me and turned off the alarm. "I don't want any interruptions," he said, his voice low.

I ran my fingers through his hair and said, "I like the way you think."

Rafe hit the shower first. I was going to start the coffee while I waited my turn, but my nose told me someone had beaten me to it.

Hilary and Webb sat at the dinette. "Good morning, sleepyhead," Webb said.

"Oh, no. Did *you* make the coffee?" I asked in dismay.

"No, I did," said Hilary.

I breathed again. "Thanks. Then it's safe to drink."

My brother rolled his eyes. "You people make wussy coffee." He looked at Hilary and said, "I'll have to teach you how to make it right."

"Thanks, but no," she said. "I've had your coffee."

I paused in the act of filling a mug. "Oh? When was this?"

"One morning when I was staying at your folks' place," she said. "Your father took one sip and dumped out the whole pot. It was hilarious."

"Banned from making coffee in my own home," Webb grumbled. "I can't wait to get my own place."

"Well, if you move in here next year, you'll still be banned from making coffee," I said. "Assuming you get accepted here. Assuming you ever get to take the ACT. What's the story on that, anyhow?"

He looked morose. "It's been rescheduled for tomorrow. Mom called me yesterday while you guys were panicking about your project."

"You're going to do fine," Hilary said, squeezing his hand.

He gave her a tight smile and went back to eating his cereal.

Rafe emerged from the hallway, putting his hair back in its customary ponytail as he walked. "Would you coffee drinkers spare a guy some hot water for tea?" he asked.

I fired up the kettle on the stove. "You'll have it in a minute," I said. Then I cocked my head and looked at his hair. "It's not fair."

"What's not fair?"

"Your hair just dips over your forehead on its own, doesn't it? I'd have to spend hours getting mine to do that."

He leaned toward me and gave me a resounding kiss on the lips. "Your hair is beautiful just the way it is."

"Eww," said Webb.

I slid my arms around Rafe's waist and looked past him toward the dinette. "What are you, six?" I said to my brother. Then I kissed my boyfriend for a long, long time.

It was snowing by the time we got to the turnoff for Grandfather's old place – just flurries, but enough to remind me of our previous disasters. As Webb maneuvered us up the rutted path, I repeated the new mantra Rafe had supplied me with that morning: Our goal wasn't to save the Earth today – our goal was to earn the gods' respect.

It was harder to believe while reminders of my past failures fell all around us.

The four of us piled out of the car and headed up the path to the cave entrance. I'd tied my scarf to a tree next to the turnoff the day before, so we wouldn't miss it. Now I worried that an animal might have made off with it in the night. But no, it was still there, fluttering in the slight breeze.

I stopped at the junction and turned to wait for the rest of the team. Rafe was right behind me. He slipped an arm around me and kissed my forehead. Hilary was next. Webb was dead last, his steps lagging as he concentrated on the fiber he was manipulating. "What's that for?" I asked.

"You'll see," he said, distracted.

The three of us exchanged a shrug. Then we all stepped onto the side path.

And stopped short at a wall where the cave entrance should have been.

I looked around for a different way in, but there was nothing – no other path, no other doorway. "Well, shit," I said. "So much for cooperation."

Rafe stepped up to the new wall and knocked. "Maybe it's a gate," he said over his shoulder. "We'd have to seal off the entrance to do the experiment anyway." There was no answer, so he knocked again. Then he pounded hard on the wall.

The wall didn't open, but Lugh materialized next to Rafe. "Sorry," He said. "Someone should have warned you that We were closing this off. I'll take you in." And without transition, we all stood inside the cave.

Hilary shifted her computer bag on her shoulder as she looked around, her eyes wide. "Wow. Y'all have been busy. I've never seen an enclosed space that was this big."

Lugh beamed. "And We have a special place just for you, Hilary," He told her. "Your Dr. Raymond is a great fellow, although a bit intimidated by Us. But We prevailed on him to allow Us to bring over all the equipment you'll need. I'll take you there now, if you're ready."

"Sure," she said.

"The rest of you sit tight," He said. And together, they disappeared.

Webb was still busy with his knitting. He was using some sort of clear filament to create a fine mesh. "What's it for?" I asked again.

"Cover for the air intake, so we don't bring in any birds or bugs. Wouldn't want you to toast them inadvertently," he said, glancing up at me with a smirk.

"That's a good idea," Rafe said. "We should have thought of that."

"That's what I'm here for," Webb said as he worked the last bit of filament and tied it off. His comment sounded more off-the-cuff than prophetic. I relaxed a bit more.

Lugh returned in a blaze of light. "That's brilliant," He said as He examined Webb's netting. "We should have thought of that." He turned to Rafe and me. "Are you ready?"

"I guess so," I said, tensing up all over again.

"Right, then, let's get you into position. Rafe and Webb, you're with Me. We'll get that net strung up over the intake in a trice. Then Rafe can start working up a wind with his wings to push the air into this chamber. Goibniu's in position at the exhaust with His bellows to help draw the cleaned air out." Goibniu, I knew, was the Celtic god of smithcraft.

Lugh pointed toward a massive pile of white powdered material on the far side of the cave. "Your quicklime supply is over there. And little Enkou's got his pond all ready to go." He pointed toward the opposite corner of the cavern's bottom, where the kappa stood at the edge of a huge basin of water. He waved up at us and winked out.

"Where's he going?" Webb asked.

"Probably to pester Hilary for cucumbers," I said. I realized I was taking shallow breaths, and concentrated on breathing more deeply. The last thing any of us needed was for me to hyperventilate and pass out.

Rafe put both hands on my shoulders. "You okay?"

"Yeah."

He tapped his forehead with a finger. "I'll be with you here."

I smiled gratefully. "I know." Then I wrapped my arms around him and held on.

He hugged me back for a few moments, and then stepped away. "Let's go," he told Lugh. He shot me an encouraging look and tapped his forehead again as they faded out.

Can you hear me? he said in my head.

I let out a breath I didn't realize I'd been holding. I really *was* going to make myself pass out if I didn't watch it. *Loud and clear,* I said. *Let's do this.* And I shifted.

I flew down to the pond and began heating the water with my eyes. Steam began to fill the vast space. I wasn't sure how hot I was making the water – I was aiming for 400 degrees Centigrade, but without a thermometer, it was hard to be precise. And as a fire being myself, it was tough to gauge how hot something else was. But it was getting hard to breathe, which I thought was a good sign. And then I noticed a white powder beginning to settle on the sloping bottom of the cavern, and realized immediately where it was coming from: the quicklime was mixing with the steam and drawing the carbon dioxide out of the ambient air in the cavern. In other words, it was working. *Okay,* I said. *Open the intake and let's see what happens.* Then I flew up to the ledge and waited.

And waited.

Is the intake open yet? I asked.

Yeah, Rafe said. *Aren't you getting any air down there?*

Not very much. The precipitate seemed to be a little thicker on the floor of the cave, but there wasn't enough of it yet to begin sliding toward the chute.

Hang on. Let me talk to Lugh.

The steam seemed to be cooling, which was going to cause a problem if condensed water mixed with the stuff on the cave floor. I flew down and began hovering over the powder. My thought was to cause a draft by beating my wings, thereby sweeping the powder down the chute and out of the cavern. It worked, after a fashion, but I couldn't keep it up forever. *What's going on?* I sent to Rafe.

We're bringing in the winds.

And seconds later, I had more air packed into the cavern than I would have thought possible. I flew back down to heat up the water again, and at last, the precipitate began sliding toward the chute under its own weight.

It's working! I cried. *Close the intake for now and let me get this much cleaned up.*

It took some time, but eventually the precipitate slowed to a trickle. *Okay, open the exhaust so we can get this batch out of here.*

Exhaust is opening, Rafe sent. And in a moment, I was tumbling toward the roof of the cavern.

A little less exhaust! I sent. *You're going to suck me out, too!* I fought against the current, finally finding shelter behind an overhang on the roof of the cavern.

Abruptly, the exhaust stopped. *Sage, are you all right?* Rafe sent. He sounded worried.

Yeah. Fine. Found shelter. I was even panting in mindspeak.

Let's take a break, he sent. *Lugh's coming in after you.*

A moment later, the ledge where I'd begun brightened as Lugh arrived. "There you are," He boomed. "Come on over here and join Me, and we'll go have a chat with the rest of the team."

I coasted across the cave, realizing – now that the imminent danger was past – how bone-tired I was. I shifted back and slumped to the floor. "All right?" Lugh asked.

"Yeah," I said wearily. "Let's get out of here." And in less than a moment, we were in a room I'd never seen before. It appeared to be some kind of control room. Hilary sat at a counter, glancing back and forth between the screen of her laptop and an array of meters before her, while she typed away on the laptop's keyboard. Enkou sat on the floor next to her, his back against the counter at her feet. He paused in his cucumber munching to wave at me. I waved back.

Webb, too, was there, seated on a spare chair to the left of the control board. He saw me on the floor and stood – intending to help me up, I suppose – but Rafe arrived just then and beat him to it. I sagged against him, grateful for his support in all senses of the word.

"How'd we do?" Rafe asked.

Hilary whirled away from her keyboard. "I didn't hear y'all come in!" she said. "Gods, Sage, you look done in."

"I am," I said. "How'd we do?"

"Y'all are not going to believe this," she said, turning back to her keyboard. "I can hardly believe it myself. But you cleaned 367 cubic kilometers of air just now of 98 percent of its CO_2." She spun back around to us. "You did it! The process worked!"

"Oh, good," I said, and passed out.

When next I opened my eyes, I was lying in my own bed. The shades were drawn, and for a minute, I thought maybe it was early morning, and I'd dreamed the whole thing in the cavern. But then I realized if that were true, my room wouldn't be packed with people the way it was now. Webb, Hilary, Mom, Dad, Rafe, and Cerridwen hovered around me, practically willing me to wake up.

I smiled weakly and held out my hand to Rafe, who took it in a convulsive grip. "What'd I miss?" I asked.

I heard the sigh of relief that went around the room. "Sage," my mother said, "if you ever scare me like that again, so help me –" Then she took the hand Rafe wasn't holding and squeezed it.

"I love you, too, Mom," I said, with a semblance of my usual snark. Then I looked up at Rafe. "So it really did work, right? I didn't dream it?"

"You didn't dream it," he said, grinning, and sat on the edge of the bed. "We were wildly successful. None of us will have to do a senior project next year. Dr. Raymond has already given us As – you, me, and Hilary. And your parents have already called Tess." He glanced their way, looking a bit irritated. "She's ready to interview us as soon as you're up for it."

I groaned. "Terrific. I could sleep for a week."

"But you can't," Hilary said. "The university administration sent an email. Classes are starting again on Monday."

I peered at her. "What day is it?"

"Today? It's still Friday."

I groaned again.

"No rest for the wicked," Webb said with a mischievous grin. Then he sobered. "Good job, sis."

"Yes, an excellent job," said Cerridwen, beaming at me. "We have learned much from this experiment. Some safeguards need to be built into the process. And We know now that it is too much to expect humans – even deity-assisted humans – to do it on their own. It's going to take all of us working together to save the Earth. And I, for one, am grateful to you for forcing Us to see that."

"You're welcome," I said, already drifting off to sleep again.

Chapter 16

Kerry showed up at last on Sunday night. We hugged, and chatted about the long break in the middle of the semester, and how unfair it was that the university was going to extend the semester into early January to make up for our weeks off.

She also accepted my apology for being such an unfeeling jerk. But even so, I could tell our friendship had turned a corner. I had a feeling that we'd never be as close again as we had been when we were kids.

Unfortunately, I was right again. Partway into the spring semester, she told me she was going to move into a house with some other psych majors. "It'll be better for me," she said. "For studying."

"Sure," I said. "That makes a lot of sense. I can't help being sad, though."

"I'm sad, too," she said. "But I think this will be better for everyone. I wouldn't be able to live here in the fall, anyway."

I knew what she was trying to say. Webb had been accepted to CU for the following school year, and of course he had first dibs on space in the house, since my parents owned it. And if he and Kerry lived under the same roof, things might get uncomfortable for all of us.

"You don't have to decide now," I said. "August is months away. You might both have moved on by then." What I didn't tell her was that Webb had already moved on. Hilary had stayed with us in Golden over our foreshortened holiday break, and the two of them seemed to be getting serious — so much so that my parents had each hauled him aside separately and advised him to go slow. Which, of course, made him even more determined to keep seeing her.

It was going to be very interesting, come fall. I expected Webb and Hilary would end up together in her room. Rafe was already in the process of moving his stuff into mine. I wondered whether I ought to look for someone to take Kerry's old room. Or maybe we'd just leave her stupid elliptical in there and use it for storage. The house was already going to be crowded with four people instead of three.

Anyway, one weekend in February, Kerry moved out. As she closed the front door for the final time, it felt very much like we were closing the door on both our childhoods.

You know the saying, "When one door closes, another opens"? The following day, Rafe officially gave up his dorm room and moved the rest of his stuff into the house. That felt less like a door opening, and more like cracking open the lid on Pandora's box. Although I supposed we had let the mischief out long since.

Another childhood door closed in March.

I dreamed I was flying, as I often did these days. I'd given up wearing the dream helmet after Rafe and my father gave me that crash course in flying. As I gained experience, I was more certain that I wouldn't wake up in a tree again – and even if I did, I was sure I would have the presence of mind to rescue myself.

Anyway, as I was flying along the Front Range in my dream, I felt an urge to land on the cliff where Grandfather had lived for so many years. There, I found him waiting for me.

I was surprised at how well he looked. Over the holidays, he had seemed shrunken into himself, spending most of his time in the rocking chair by our kitchen fireplace. But in my dream, he was hale and healthy – much as he must have looked before Loki attacked him the first time. I called his name and ran to him.

"You are all grown up, granddaughter," he said, his voice strong, as he returned my hug. "You have met your challenges well this year. The gods are pleased with you, and so am I."

"It was really hard," I confessed. "There were so many times I thought I'd never make it. But Rafe was there to help me. And Mom and Dad and Webb and Hilary, of course," I added quickly, "and you, too."

"Ah, Sage," he said with a chuckle. "You are kind to an old man. I regret I wasn't able to do more to help you."

"You're always a help," I said. "Just knowing you're there – knowing I can turn to you – is the biggest help of all."

He smiled, but didn't reply directly. Instead, he said, "Rafe is a fine young warrior."

I snorted softly. "Yeah. Just what I needed – another Trickster in my life. As if Dad and Webb weren't enough." Then I softened my tone. "I'm in love with him, Grandfather."

"I know," he said.

"Is he...?" I didn't know why I was asking him. As far as I knew, Grandfather had only ever had one prophetic vision – the one about White Buffalo Calf Pipe Woman and Mom. If I wanted to know my future, I ought to have been asking Webb.

"Does he love you?" he said, finishing my question, and nodded. "Yes, he does. But you know that."

"I guess." I ducked my head.

"As to whether he is the man you will spend your life with?" He shrugged. "I can't tell you that. All I can say is that he is a good man, and you seem well-suited."

Warmth bloomed in my belly. "I think so, too."

He grunted. Then he hugged me again. "I will always be with you, granddaughter." And then he released me and turned away.

"Grandfather?" I followed him as he approached the edge of the cliff. "What are you doing? Be careful!"

He turned back to me and said, with a twinkle in his eye, "I am always careful." Then he stepped off the edge of the precipice and began walking up into the sky.

"Grandfather!"

But he was gone.

I came awake to my phone ringing. I already knew what it meant.

We buried him in the mountain meadow that he had protected for so long. Everyone came – Aunt Shannon and Uncle George,

Charlie and Winnie Frank, Grandpa Drew and Grandma, my Uncle Thom and Aunt Hannah and their family, and elders of both the Ute and Lakota tribes who I only knew in passing.

The gods, too, came to honor him for the last time. White Buffalo Calf Pipe Woman called him her best and bravest warrior.

Dad clung to Mom, looking like he'd lost his anchor. Mom herself looked hollow-eyed. "I don't know what I'm going to do now," I heard her say to Aunt Shannon. "Looks Far was our rock."

"You'll go on," Aunt Shannon said. "He'd want you to. And you know he'll always be with us."

One good thing came from Grandfather's death – Uncle George finally proposed to Aunt Shannon, and she said yes. "Life doesn't go on forever, Sage," he said when I congratulated him. "I don't know how many times Looks Far told me that, but I was too pig-headed to listen to him. And look at all the time I've wasted." He shook his head at himself.

"Anyway, I'm sure he's thrilled right now," I said.

He snorted. "I bet he's laughing his ass off at me."

"That, too," I said.

We were able to keep the success of Rafe's project under wraps for several months. No one ever asked me to go into that cavern again, for which I was grateful. Instead, our demonstration project seemed to serve to show the gods how it needed to be done. They found a different heat source, mostly using solar power, and Hilary, Rafe, and I were relegated to roles as monitors.

It was only when the agencies of several governments around the world began to notice a substantial drop in atmospheric CO_2 levels that the university came clean, so to speak, about what was going on. That led to about a zillion requests for interviews. But of course, we'd promised the exclusive to NWNN.

Tess and Schuyler brought their traveling dog-and-pony show up to the monitoring station, and we did the interview with an impressive backdrop of meters and switches and computer equipment. Rafe explained the process in layman's terms, and I obligingly shifted so Schuyler could get some shots of the firebird swooping through the air. Even the elusive Enkou consented to a cameo, after Tess bribed him with a sufficient number of cucumbers.

Our campus celebrity had died down after the big snowstorm bumped us out of the headlines. But once our latest interview with Tess aired, it came roaring back in full force. Rafe enjoyed the attention at first, but he rapidly got sick of running a gantlet of shrieking women every time he left the house to go to class. I complained to Dad, who suggested hiring a security guard. "Or we could install an electric fence," he said, only half-serious.

"Great," I said. "We'd be living in a gulag. There must be another way."

It was Cerridwen who solved the problem for us. She engaged the services of a banshee, who wailed like a siren only when a group of people gathered on our sidewalk for more than ten minutes – and who could only be heard by the people in that group. After about a week, the crowds dispersed, and we had no further trouble with either tourists or fans.

When I thanked Her, She waved me off. "Tch. It's the least I could do for the team that saved the Earth."

"All we did was show You how to do it," I protested.

"And lit a fire under Us. Your family seems to have a talent for that."

"That," I told Her, "is totally my mother's fault."

Author's Note

I ended up very annoyed at Sage, Rafe, and Hilary by the end of this book. I've been out of college for decades, and my science classes back then had nothing to do with climate change. But these three forced me to look more closely at the issue, and to try to understand some of the science involved.

I mentioned in a blog post while I was writing this book that if there was one thing that really cheesed me off in connection with climate change, it was this: We will not be able to reverse it until we begin to pull greenhouse gases, particularly carbon dioxide, out of the atmosphere and put them back into the Earth. But we're not funding much research into carbon sequestration. It's not that we don't know how to do it; scientists know of a number of ways, including the quicklime process Rafe proposes in this book. But these projects just can't get enough funding. Why? Because the potential backers – the people with the money – don't want to fund anything that won't give them a return on their investment. Never mind that life on Earth as we know it is hanging in the balance; if a project can't make money for its investors, it's not worth doing.

It all seems so short-sighted to me.

[The author climbs down from her soapbox and puts it away.]

Kudos as usual go to Susan Strayer, my editor, and Kat Milyko, my beta reader. They continue to provide me with Japanese translation assistance and on-point editorial advice. Thanks, ladies.

For *Firebird's Snare* as for *Dragon's Web*, I found *Climate Change: What It Means for Us, Our Children, and Our Grandchildren,* edited by Joseph F.C. DiMento and Pamela Doughman, to be helpful as a reference. Also, *Shamans and Kushtakas: North Coast Tales of the Supernatural* by Mary Giraudo Beck was my major source for information about kushtakas.

To get the first word on all of my new releases, please sign up for my spam-free newsletter. I'll also post the info at my blog and on my Facebook page, but the newsletter is your guaranteed way to find out what's coming up.

One more thing: If you enjoyed *Firebird's Snare* – or even if you didn't – won't you please go back where you purchased the book to post a review? Reviews are a key way that readers find good books, and I treasure each and every review that my books receive. Thank you in advance!

Lynne Cantwell
June 2015

About the Author

Lynne Cantwell writes mostly urban fantasy and paranormal romance, with a dash of magic realism when she's feeling more serious. She is also a contributing author for Indies Unlimited. In a previous life, she was a broadcast journalist who worked at Mutual/NBC Radio News, CNN, and a bunch of other places you have probably never heard of. She has a master's degree in fiction writing from Johns Hopkins University. Currently, she lives near Washington, D.C.

Discover other titles by Lynne Cantwell:

The Maidens' War
SwanSong
Seasons of the Fool

The Pipe Woman Chronicles:
Seized
Fissured
Tapped
Gravid
Annealed
The Pipe Woman Chronicles Omnibus

Land, Sea, Sky:
Where Were You When: An Anthology
Crosswind
Undertow
Scorched Earth
The Land, Sea, Sky Trilogy

The Pipe Woman's Legacy:
Dragon's Web
Firebird's Snare

Indies Unlimited 2012 Flash Fiction Anthology (contributor)
Indies Unlimited 2013 Flash Fiction Anthology (contributor)

Indies Unlimited Tutorials and Tools for Prospering in a Digital World (contributor)
Indies Unlimited Tutorials and Tools for Prospering in a Digital World, Vol. II (contributor)
BookGoodies How to Write A Book (contributor)
First Chapters (contributor)
13 Bites (contributor)
Summer Dreams (contributor)
Boo!: Volume 2 (contributor)
Winter Tales (contributor)
Plan 559 from Outer Space (contributor)

Find Lynne on Teh Intarwebz:

Facebook: http://www.facebook.com/pages/Lynne-Cantwell
Twitter: http://twitter.com/lynnecantwell
Google Plus: http://plus.google.com/+LynneCantwell
Goodreads:
http://www.goodreads.com/author/show/696603.Lynne_Cantwell
Blog: http://www.hearth-myth.com

Sage and Webb's mother did write her memoirs!
Here's the first chapter of the book that started it all:

Seized

Book One of the Pipe Woman Chronicles

The e-book edition is FREE at all major online booksellers!

~~~

You know how they say you should be careful what you wish for? Well, I'm living proof.

Let's start with the night Brock proposed to me. We met as law students, in the same class at the University of Denver, and now we worked at the same big law firm in town. He was a counsel and on track to make partner, a rising star in the firm. I too should have been about to make partner, but I had deliberately shifted my career along a different course. After a couple of years of working on big client cases, I became disillusioned with both the document review drudgery that new associates get stuck doing, and the cutthroat adversarial nature of most legal matters. So I went for mediation training. It meant going half-time at the firm while I earned certificates in both mediation and alternative dispute resolution, but the firm graciously agreed to allow me to complete my mediation internship there. I sold the management committee on the idea that having a certified mediator on staff would bring us business. They were dubious to start with, and I got plenty of advice about how I was derailing my "promising career as a litigator." But now that a couple of years had passed, the partners were beginning to trust me and my methods, and were starting to throw business my way.

Just that week, I had completed an arbitration for a dicey matter involving the owners of a local sports team and their star player, and Brock insisted that we go to Colt & Gray to celebrate. He seemed as thrilled as I was that the alternative dispute resolution (or ADR) had gone so well, although he seemed most thrilled that the team owners, who were clients of our firm on some other matters, had gotten nearly everything they wanted.

"But the player got what he wanted, too," I insisted as the waiter placed our food before us. Brock had chosen the grilled beef hearts with marrow butter. He had tried to persuade me to order the same thing – "it would be so appropriate, considering the way you eviscerated the other guys," he'd said – but I picked the seared salmon instead. "And there are no 'other guys' in mediation, Brock," I continued. "You know that."

"Sure, sure," he said, waving one hand airily before slicing into his meat.

I watched him for a few seconds before reaching for my own utensils, marveling again at how I had landed the guy. Brock Holt was the quintessential jock – tall, broad-shouldered and slim-hipped, with the blond hair and perpetual tan of the die-hard skier. He had confided in me at one point in law school that he was drawn to the profession initially because it seemed to have a massive potential for doing business on the slopes; that the actual practice of law fit his aggressive personality was a nice plus.

Okay, not aggressive – ruthless. Brock could be quite the bastard, given half a chance. And his practice gave him more than half a chance. He had been counseled more than once to go easy on his bulldog style, but not very seriously; some of the partners appreciated playing the good cop to Brock's bad cop.

So what was Naomi Witherspoon doing with him, anyway? I had heard the talk around the office about how Naomi the Nice – the girl with the pale face, the one who wore hippie clothes to hide her extra pounds and had that weird conciliatory vibe – didn't belong with Brock the Bastard. And yet we'd been dating since our final year of law school. Brock had stuck by me during my professional dark night of the soul, and was one of my biggest boosters professionally.

Oh sure, we'd had our ups and downs. We had broken up more than once, usually over his penchant for flirting with the female baby associates. He always swore that they came on to him – which I could almost believe, except that I'd seen him come on to them right back. But all that seemed to be in the past now; we hadn't had a major dust-up for at least a couple of years, and I had begun to think that maybe he was ready to settle down.

God knows *I* was ready to settle down. We were both past thirty and my biological clock was ticking ever louder. We were becoming established in our careers, we were comfortable with one another, we had plenty of money – why not get married and have kids?

"Something wrong with the salmon?" he asked, gesturing at my plate with his knife.

"Oh!" I glanced down, realizing that while I'd been lost in my reverie, he had torn through half of his entree. "Sorry. No, nothing's wrong with it. I was just thinking again about how well the ADR went." No way would I tell him I'd been thinking about how good he looked. His ego didn't need any encouragement. "How's your heart?"

"Terrific, as always," he grinned before popping another piece into his mouth. Then he sat back and said, "You're really on a roll lately. The Bingham estate settlement, that copyright infringement matter, and now this."

I waved off the compliment with a self-deprecatory smile. "I'm having fun. I get to learn a little bit about a lot of different areas of law. Beats the hell out of document review." I wrinkled my nose in disgust at the thought as I took a bite of the salmon, then smiled appreciatively as I chewed.

"Sure," Brock continued, "but that's not what I meant. It's like you have a knack for persuasion."

"Like you have a knack for intimidation?" I asked with a sardonic grin. Really, we're pretty well matched – I can be a bastard sometimes, too.

He rolled his eyes. "You know what I mean. Like you have a magic talent or something. Ross told Perry that it was like he couldn't help agreeing with everything you said."

I had been about to stab into my fish for another bite, but my fork stalled just above the plate as I stared at him. "Ross shouldn't even be speaking to Perry about the ADR."

Conflict of interest, in a law firm setting, is a funny bird. There's a seemingly inexhaustible supply of clients, and a big client can have hundreds of matters, but there are only so many law firms. Inevitably, a client will run into a situation where its go-to law firm also represents its opponent. At that point, a virtual wall can be erected within the firm to keep the lawyers assigned to matter A ignorant of what's going on in matter B, and vice versa. The system works, but only if everybody involved scrupulously plays along.

"Don't worry," Brock said hastily, "Ross didn't give away any details about the settlement. Since he was in the building, he stopped by Perry's office to talk about the training camp lease. Perry told me he was making small talk with Ross — you know, 'how's it going in general,' that kind of thing — and Ross volunteered that you seemed to have a magic touch. He meant it as a compliment. Don't get sore."

I thought about it for a second. "Yeah, I guess that's okay," I conceded, and took that bite of salmon. "I shouldn't look a gift horse in the mouth, huh?" I continued ruefully. "I should be grateful for a client to put in a good word for me with a partner, especially since promotion evals are coming up."

Brock grinned. "Exactly." He jumped, and then looked abashed. "Forgot to take my phone off vibrate," he apologized, pulling the offending device from the pocket of his slacks. He glanced at the number and got up from the table. "I've got to take this in private, sorry."

I nodded and gestured at my plate. "Go," I said. "It'll give me a chance to catch up to you." He grinned and walked away, putting the phone to his ear as he went. I propped my chin on my free hand for a moment, watching the tails of his suit jacket move as he walked and imagining the play of muscle underneath. Then he rounded a corner and I went back to my cooling dinner.

He was right about my string of successes. For the past month or so, I had been pleasantly surprised by the ease in which I was settling cases. Experience counted for some of it, of course. But every case was different, and no amount of experience can prepare you for the twists and turns that some matters take. Even as I tallied my wins and basked in my success, a little voice in my head kept asking whether things weren't coming too easily, whether I wasn't heading for a hard fall.

It's true: my mother didn't raise any self-confident children. The only child she raised, in fact, was me. She had carefully instilled in me a Protestant work ethic; a strong streak of humility; and the sense that what God giveth, God could taketh away on a whim.

The boyfriend, I was pretty sure, I got on my own. But God could taketh him away if I didn't locketh him down pretty damn soon.

I saw Brock re-enter the dining room and murmured, "Why don't you just ask me to marry you already?"

His eyes widened for an instant. Then he nodded once, decisively. Smiling broadly, he resumed his seat and reached for my hand. "Listen," he said, "you're not going home for Christmas, are you?"

I blinked. "I hadn't planned on it. I've got a couple of mediations after New Year's to get ready for, and I've got to finish drafting the ADR order. Why?"

"Why don't we go skiing? We've got the condo in Vail. Days on the mountain, evenings before the fire, nights...." His grin became almost predatory. "What do you say?"

"*We've* got a condo in Vail?" I asked, amused. "*You've* got a condo in Vail."

"But it will be ours after I put your name on it."

"After...?"

"After we're married."

He had stunned me for the second time that evening. "Are you proposing to me?" I said in disbelief.

He glanced around, still holding tightly to my hand. "It's not the most romantic setting, I know, but I'll get down on one knee if you want me to. Maybe we'd get a free bottle of champagne out of it." He half-rose from his chair, his napkin slipping to the floor.

I laughed delightedly. "That is completely unnecessary. Sit back down, you goofball."

"You're sure?" he asked, still in a crouch.

"Yes!" I snatched back my hand and bent over to get his napkin, still laughing.

"Yes, you're sure? Or yes, you'll marry me?"

I searched his gaze. Then I said, with all the honesty I could muster, "I love you, Brock. I've loved you for years. But I've never really been sure whether you loved me, too."

His face softened, and tenderness shone from his eyes. "If I didn't love you, why would I ask you to marry me?"

That wasn't exactly the phrasing I was after, but I decided it would do for now. "Yes, Brock, I will marry you," I said, smiling.

He whooped and waved over the waiter with a grand gesture. "A bottle of your best champagne for the happy couple," he said, loud enough for everyone in the restaurant to hear. "We're engaged!" The place erupted in applause.

We skipped dessert and went to my place. I lit a fire in my bedroom fireplace (I fell in love with the condo precisely because it had fireplaces in both the great room and the bedroom) and we proceeded to, in Brock's elegant phrasing, consummate our engagement. But then I sent him home. I don't know why, exactly; he had certainly spent the night before. But I realized that tonight, I wanted the place to myself. So as the fire log in the grate sputtered out, I pleaded exhaustion and sent him on his way, blowing him a kiss from my doorway as he stepped onto the elevator.

I closed the door behind me and leaned against it. Then I glanced into the mirror that I'd put by the door for last-minute appearance checks (and usually forgot to use) and noted the spots of color on my cheeks and the smile that hadn't left my face since Brock proposed. *My face is gonna hurt in the morning from all this unaccustomed smiling.* I laughed aloud at the thought.

Then I got myself a glass of water and a couple of acetaminophen. No way I was going to start my new life as a fiancée with a hangover.

I wasn't sleepy, despite the alcohol and the exercise. I toyed with the TV remote for a minute or two, then reached for my cell phone and called my best friend Shannon to give her the good news.

"Naomi?" she answered. "I was just going to bed. What's up?"

"Ms. McDonough," I said grandly, "you have the honor and pleasure of addressing the future Mrs. Brock Holt!"

"I knew it!" she crowed. I could visualize her in her Day of the Dead jammies, her auburn curls cropped close from the wretched haircut she'd gotten over the weekend and her face alight with glee.

"You did not!" I said. "How could you have? It was a complete surprise to me."

"There was a disturbance in the ether," she said smugly, and I pshawed in disbelief. Shannon claimed to be fey, but I didn't buy most of her New Agey woo-woo stuff. She always struck me as simply very observant of others' emotional states, which was a big help to her in her job as a social worker. I often took mental note of her techniques and then used them in my mediation practice. (I'd confessed it to her once, and asked if it was okay with her; she claimed to have known about it all along.)

"And where is Mr. Holt?" she asked.

"I sent him home."

"Ah," she said mysteriously.

"What the hell does 'ah' mean?" I asked.

"Oh, nothing," she said.

"You're a rotten liar, Shannon."

She laughed. "So you're going to go to bed alone, then?"

"I have to work in the morning!" I protested. "I can't stay up all night having sex!" As her laughter died down, I added, "Anyway, there will be plenty of time for that next week. Brock invited me to his condo in the mountains for Christmas. You know, skiing, ring shopping, long nights by the fireplace. That sort of thing."

"Well, congratulations," she said. "It's been a long time coming. I thought he'd never ask you. What did your mother say?"

My smile faded. "Haven't called her yet."

"Ah," Shannon said again.

"Would you quit with the 'ah'?" I demanded. "Anyway, I wasn't planning to go home for Christmas – I was going to stay here and work, remember?"

"Of course I remember. But I also know she's not that wild about Brock."

"Mostly, she's been wondering why he's been taking so long to propose," I said. "She should love him to pieces now."

"Mmm," she said.

"That's no better than 'ah,'" I told her. "Look, I don't think I'll be able to sleep. Why don't I come over? I've got a plate of cookies my secretary gave me for Christmas. I'll bring them along – you can help me eat them."

"Are they that bad?" she laughed.

"No, they're terrific. But if I eat them all myself, Brock may think twice about marrying Naomi the Whale."

"You should have asked him to help you eat them," she said. "Then you could begin to grow old and fat together. Okay, come on over. I'll put the kettle on."

"See you in ten minutes," I said, and hung up. Then I grabbed the cookies from the kitchen counter and headed to the basement garage.

Shannon lived in a triplex north of Sloan's Lake, only ten minutes or so from my loft in LoDo (the nickname for Denver's trendy, if I do say so myself, Lower Downtown neighborhood). It was a Wednesday night so traffic should have been light, but the bars were closing and the crowd was clogging up the streets. Working my ginger Nissan Cube free of LoDo at last, I pulled up behind a car that was sitting at a stop sign...and sitting...and sitting. No traffic was coming in either direction that I could see, and my earlier ebullient mood was evaporating by the second. Finally, in frustration, I cried out, "Just go, already!"

The car ahead leaped into the intersection. A horn blared as another car shot into my range of vision from the left, narrowly missing the first car. As the driver on the cross street flew by, still honking, the other driver rocked to a halt on the other side of the intersection and just sat there.

I realized my hand was covering my mouth. I pulled it away with an effort and sat for a moment, glancing between the flaring brake lights across the road and my hands trembling on the steering wheel. Finally, the other car's brake lights went out and he, or she, drove away. Slowly and carefully, I did the same.

Shannon met me at the door, her grin dissolving into a look of concern. She snatched the cookies as if she was afraid I would drop them, then took my coat and steered me to the wicker loveseat. An opened novel sat, flipped over, on the coffee table, atop a pile of papers. She removed the aluminum foil covering the cookies and set chamomile teabags to steep in two mugs with a matching Navajo design. Then, finally, she said, "What happened?"

I told her. About the other driver, and about the settlements.

As I talked, my brain began clicking things into place. It wasn't just that I was getting really good at my job – it *was* too easy. People were far too suggestible around me. The client had told Perry that I had a magic touch. That he couldn't help agreeing with everything I said.

I could tell someone to get out of my way at an intersection, even if it put that person in danger.

"Something weird is going on," I finished, rather lamely.

"Yes, it is," Shannon agreed. "And now you know what the 'ah' meant."

I blinked. "On the phone?" I tried to sip my tea, burned my lip and swore.

"Sorry, it's hot," she said, and fetched an ice cube for me. "Suck on that. Yes, on the phone. I've always sensed an odd aura around you, but it's gotten worse over the past month or so."

"Worse?"

"Stronger," she amended. "Worse is a value judgment. I'm not prepared to make a value judgment at this time."

The ice cube felt good against my sore lip, but the melt water was dripping down my wrist. I dropped what was left of the cube into my mug and wiped my wrist on my jeans. "Okay," I said carefully, afraid we were veering into the woo-woo. "When will you be prepared?"

She laughed. "I know you don't believe in the supernatural, Naomi, and some of it, you're right to doubt. But a lot of it is real." She reached under the novel and extracted a green handbill from atop the pile. Then she handed it to me. "We should go to that." She bit into a chocolate cookie and sighed. "Your secretary makes good cookies."

I nodded in agreement as I nibbled at a star-shaped sugar cookie covered in yellow sprinkles and glanced over the sheet. Then I put the cookie down. "Oh, Shannon, come on," I said, looking squarely at her. "You can't be serious."

"I am serious," she said. "These cookies are delicious. And we really should go to this sweat."

I looked at the handbill again. It advertised a "special Winter Solstice 2012 sweat lodge" up in the mountains near Boulder on Friday – two days away. "By invitation only," it said.

"We're not invited," I said, tossing the paper atop her novel.

"We are," she countered. "That's the invitation."

"Well," I said, "*I'm* not invited. I'd have to take off work, and I'm already planning to take next week off to go to Vail with Brock."

"Actually," Shannon said, "you *are* invited. An Indian guy dropped off the invitation at my office today as I was seeing a client out. He said specifically that it was for you and me."

My head snapped up. "What?"

"He said he knew you."

"He specifically said to you, 'Shannon, this is for you and Naomi'?"

She shrugged. "Not exactly in those words, but yes, he mentioned you by name."

I shook my head in disbelief. "He must have me confused with someone else. I don't know any Indians. Not well enough to be invited to a ceremony, anyway." I picked up the handbill again. "Is this going to be authentic?"

"I think so," she said. "Wait. What do you mean by 'authentic'?"

"Native American Church-type authentic. Including peyote."

She shrugged. "I don't know. But if it's a bad scene, we'll leave."

"You can count on that," I said, and then thought of another objection. "You're not trying to sucker me into some goofy Age of Aquarius, end-of-the-world thing, are you? Real Indians are running this, not one of those New Age charlatans?"

Shannon's eyes had narrowed as I spoke, but she answered me. "The guy who gave me the invitation seemed authentic enough to me."

"What did he look like?"

"Well, he wasn't dressed in buckskin and fringe, with feathers in his hair, if that's what you're asking."

I dialed it back a bit. "I'm not making fun of you, honest. I'm just worried about us ending up like the people who died in that bogus sweat lodge ceremony in Arizona a few years back. Really, what did he look like?"

She dropped her hackles a little. "A jacket over a plaid Western shirt," she said. "Jeans. Boots, but work boots – not expensive cowboy boots." Her eyes unfocused as she recalled details. "It was his face that sold me. He was dark-skinned and had those Indian features, you know? And long, dark hair, like yours. He had it pulled back in a ponytail and braided." Her eyes refocused on me. "But his eyes were bright blue."

"And he said he knew me."

She nodded. I shook my head. No blue-eyed Indians were coming to mind.

"Look, Naomi," she said. "I see it this way. You already know weird stuff is happening to you. And on the same day you figure this out, a strange man invites us to a Native American ceremony. Maybe he has some answers for you." And she said again, "If it gets too weird, we'll leave."

I sighed. "Okay, fine, let's go, I guess." I read over the paper again, so I didn't have to see the satisfied look on Shannon's face. "This thing starts at sundown. That's, what, 4:30 in the afternoon? And the light will fade sooner on this side of the mountains. I'll leave work at noon and pick you up at your office. We can grab lunch on the way."

"No lunch," she said. "We'll be fasting."

"Maybe *you'll* be fasting," I said, "but *I'm* going to eat lunch. I don't do woo-woo on an empty stomach."

I drove home, careful to keep my opinions about the other drivers on the road to myself.

It was after one in the morning by the time I got back to my loft. I was in that weird state of keyed-up exhaustion in which you're never sure whether you'll be able to fall asleep. But the alarm was going to go off at 6:30 a.m., regardless, so I decided to give it a try.

No sooner had my head hit the pillow than I started to dream. Or at least it seemed like a dream.

I was about twelve. I was wearing a fluffy white coat that Mom had bought for me when I was in sixth grade, and my hair hung in braided pigtails behind my ears. I could hear someone droning on about some Indian legend. I turned away from the voice, and came face to face with a small, white buffalo. His withers came even with my eyes, and he didn't have any horns. I reached out to touch his fur – I think I intended to pet him, like you would a dog – but his front half dropped to the ground, his skinny legs stuck out straight in front of him, while his back half stayed up in the air. The droning voice stopped, and then cried, "He bowed to her! The white buffalo calf bowed to her!" I heard more voices then, murmuring behind me. The little buffalo's rump then sank to the ground, and as I bent to try to touch his head once more, I looked up.

Behind the buffalo stood a woman. Her dress was made of white buckskin, elaborately fringed along the seams of the bodice and sleeves. Her hair – long, straight, and black as night – fell around her shoulders like a cloak. Her skin was deeply tanned; her eyes were black and kind, and their depths went on forever. And she was smiling at me, and nodding. She seemed to be encouraging me to touch the little buffalo calf, which still lay motionless at my feet.

The voices behind me were approaching. My hand was a fraction of an inch from the buffalo calf's head when a crow began to squawk. I looked up again, glancing around for the crow, who continued to squawk insistently. Repeatedly. Regularly.

Groaning, I rolled over and hit the snooze button to silence the alarm. But I didn't go back to sleep. Instead, I lay there, wide awake and staring up at the ceiling, remembering.

I'd forgotten about that white coat, and about how Mom used to put my hair in pigtails. And I had totally forgotten about that field trip in seventh grade to see the legendary white buffalo calf that had been born over the summer.

We lived in Logansport, Indiana, then, and the buffalo calf was born on a farm in Kewanna, a bend in the road nearby. We rode a school bus to the farm. I remembered using a fingernail to scrape away the frost flowers that had bloomed overnight on the inside of the bus window. Or maybe that was a different bus on another morning. I rode a bus every day to school, growing up. Anyway, it was cold that morning, and frosty, but we hadn't had any snow yet.

I'd forgotten how bored I'd become at the spiel the farmer gave our class about the white buffalo calf legend. I had been in the back of the group so it was hard to hear, and I was getting cold, standing in one spot. So I wandered away, down the dirt path to the corral.

I remembered, now, spying the white calf with his mother near the barn, and propping my forearms on the fence railing to watch them together — my own private showing of the miracle calf. And then the calf saw me, and came over. And — how could I have forgotten this? — the little buffalo had indeed dropped to the ground in front of me.

There was a big to-do when the farmer spotted us, just as there had been in my dream, and my teacher made a big deal about it when we got back to school. The kids on the bus called me "Indian girl" and "buffalo girl" for months afterward, all through that winter, during which I had to keep wearing that damned white coat because Mom couldn't afford to get me a different one. But she stopped putting my hair in braids after that. And at the end of the school year, we moved to Lafayette, a bigger town. By the time I started classes at my new school in the fall, everyone had forgotten about the miracle calf and the girl it had supposedly bowed to — and even if they remembered, there was nothing in Lafayette to connect it to me.

But how had *I* forgotten?

And why had there been an Indian woman in my dream, when none had been there in real life?

www.ingramcontent.com/pod-product-compliance
Lightning Source LLC
Chambersburg PA
CBHW071242130626
46556CB00003B/1127